Each of Us a Universe

Jeanne Zulick Ferruolo
with Ndengo Gladys Mwilelo

FARRAR STRAUS GIROUX
NEW YORK

Farrar Straus Giroux Books for Young Readers
An imprint of Macmillan Children's Publishing Group, LLC
120 Broadway, New York, NY 10271 • mackids.com

Our books may be purchased in bulk for promotional, educational,
or business use. Please contact your local bookseller or the Macmillan
Corporate and Premium Sales Department at (800) 221-7945 ext. 5442
or by email at MacmillanSpecialMarkets@macmillan.com.

Library of Congress Control Number: 2021025252

First edition, 2022
Designed by Michelle Gengaro-Kokmen
Printed in the United States of America by Lakeside Book Company,
Harrisonburg, Virginia

ISBN 978-0-374-38868-3 (hardcover)
1 3 5 7 9 10 8 6 4 2

For Ndengo Gladys Mwilelo,
a teacher to many,
and
for anyone facing their own mountain—
hold on

There's as many atoms in a single molecule of
your DNA as there are stars in the typical galaxy.
We are, each of us, a little universe.

—Neil deGrasse Tyson,
Cosmos: A Spacetime Odyssey

Each of Us a Universe

Chapter 1

For Calliope Scott, two things mattered: the mountain and her mother.

There was a time when she thought they were made of the same stuff.

Sturdy stuff. Unbreakable stuff.

Even magical stuff.

But ever since that September day when everything changed, Cal knew they weren't, and the only thing left to do was run to the one she believed could save the other.

Now, more than a month later, she was still running.

As the doors of Bleaker K–8's bus #3 *slowly* folded open, Cal cradled her casted arm and leapt over the bus's three steps, landing on Mountain Road with a defiant "Oomph!"

"Slow down, Cal!" the bus driver called. But Cal didn't hear . . . or care anyway. Without pausing, she set her chin against the cool October breeze and ran even harder.

Her feet barely touched the ground as she raced past Demsky's Market. Her backpack propelled her forward with urgent *pat, pat, pat*s.

Crickets hidden inside tall brown grass cheered her on. *Katy did, Katy didn't, Katy did.* The louder they sang, the harder Cal ran, sending a flurry of dead leaves swirling in her wake.

She dashed past the three houses—green, blue, brown—as the pavement steepened, then narrowed, then turned to dirt in front of the rusted, yellow sign that read

Welcome to Mount Meteorite
Bleakerville's Hidden Magic
Elevation 2,019 feet

Without pausing, she slapped the sign a high five, leaving its gong-like vibration behind her as she ducked beneath the forest canopy.

Although the well-worn trail veered left, Cal shot

right, pivoting around pines and over brambles until the path turned rocky and rugged.

When she came to the place where just one more step would send her tumbling, she turned to face the mountain's ledge. She hugged its cool granite with her unbroken arm. Then—balancing on the outside edges of her boots— she shimmied sideways across its pencil-thin ridge until she reached the boulder outside Wildcat's cave.

There she stood.

Panting and red-faced.

A pulse of electricity beat inside her temples.

She greedily inhaled the musky smells of moldy leaves and dirt. Scents only the mountain itself could have exhaled in a long, deep sigh.

From halfway up the mountain, Cal had two clear views: the place she was running to and the one she was running from.

She fixed her gaze on the first, Mount Meteorite's spire—a one-hundred-foot-tall monolith that grew from the mountain like a stone skyscraper. Made of quartz and granite, the spire formed the mountain's highest point. Each afternoon, the setting sun hit its peak in a way that made it look like a flaming matchstick. This phenomenon only served to fuel its legend of mystery and magic.

The second, and far less interesting, view was of the

tiny town of Bleakerville, the place where Cal had lived her whole life. It reminded her of an old-fashioned post-card, faded and worn and ripped at the edges.

Cal easily found her own mold-green house, with its crooked roof and sagging shutters. Next to that was Mr. and Mrs. Demsky's tidy blue cottage, with its ginger-bread trim and thread of smoke coming from its chimney. Then came the vacant brown carriage house that the elderly couple lent out now and again.

She let her gaze travel down Mountain Road to her bus stop in front of Demsky's Market and on to Main Street, where she found the tall steeple of the Congregational church and the synagogue's rounded dome. Beyond that, Bleaker K–8 School stretched sideways in a dull brick rect-angle, and the run-down New England Glass factory sat boarded and empty. There was a time when almost every-one in town had worked at the factory, but since it went bankrupt during the pandemic, its doors remained shut.

Cal sighed. Autumn used to bring comfort. Cool, crisp air and brightly colored leaves. Cozy sweaters and stacked cordwood. But ever since *the day when every-thing changed*, her family—her world—had become as broken as her town.

She hugged her casted arm, then turned her gaze once more toward the spire and the magic she knew it held.

She jumped down from the boulder, onto the rock platform, before ducking into the cave.

Inside, her eyes slowly adjusted to the dark as she made her way to the back. Surrounded by granite, she let her body absorb its damp earth smells of mold and lichen and decaying leaves. She pulled out a flashlight, directing its beam at the piles of supplies.

First, the ones she'd brought on earlier trips. A dented pot, mess kit, eating utensils, an extra pair of hiking boots, a pile of dry socks, a sleeping bag with a hole in it, carabiners, climbing rope, tin snips, and five cans of baked beans. Next to that, the equipment she'd found in June when she'd first discovered the cave. Aluminum cups, belay devices, a piton hammer, and several small burlap bags marked GEOLOGICAL SURVEY SAMPLE. She touched each item as if greeting an old friend.

Then she froze.

Sitting on a large flat rock by itself was something Cal had never seen before. It was a brown wooden box, no bigger than a shoe and shaped like a half-moon.

Cal racked her brain, trying to remember putting it there. But of course, she hadn't. She had no idea what it was.

Her skin prickled with distrust as she hugged her casted arm and inched closer.

She knew the box hadn't walked there by itself. Someone must have brought it. But who? She'd never seen anyone on the mountain, and no one else would dare navigate the skinny ridge that led to the cave.

She shined the flashlight's beam around the rest of the cave. Nothing else had been disturbed. Even the dead leaves that lined its entrance seemed untouched.

Squatting in front of the box, Cal's eyes grew large. She let her backpack slip from her shoulder.

With her good arm, she reached for a stick and poked the box as if it were a sleeping snake. Then she gently flicked open its lid.

There was something inside.

She leaned over and lifted out a white handkerchief. Stitched into the cloth in shiny green and gold letters was one word:

AMANI.

A rustling noise at the cave's entrance set the hairs on the back of Cal's neck on end. She sprang to her feet, spinning to face the intruder.

Two yellow eyes glowed inside the dim cave.

"Wildcat!" Cal's forehead wrinkled. She placed her good hand on her hip. "I've been worried about you!"

The Maine Coon cat sauntered toward her. His unruly black fur jutted in every direction. His left ear pointed at attention while the right one flopped tiredly. His tail bent in a broken angle, sweeping the ground behind him. Prickers and dead leaves clung to his body like armor. He brushed against Cal's leg.

"I haven't seen you for two days." Cal shook her head sternly. "Look at you! What have you been into?" She pried a stick from his gnarled tail.

Wildcat nosed her backpack.

"Yes, yes, of course I brought it. I think you only find me when you're hungry." Cal unzipped the backpack and pulled out a bright yellow tin can that she peeled open. The smell of fish erupted inside the musty cave. She knelt, dumping oily sardines into her hand, then held them out as an offering. Wildcat leaned in and gobbled.

"Slower. You're going to make yourself sick."

When there was nothing left, the cat licked Cal's palm. "You need to take better care of yourself."

She wiped her hand on her jeans, then began to pluck burrs and leaves from his tangled fur. "So, what do *you* know about this box?"

Wildcat answered with his usual gurgly-purr.

She squinted at the note. "And what is this? Is it even a word? Or some kind of clue?" she asked. "Do you think it has to do with the magic meteorite that fell on the spire?"

Wildcat blinked.

Cal nodded. "Me too."

She pulled a notebook from her backpack and copied the word, then returned the cloth to its box, carefully replacing its cover. She made her way back to the cave's entrance.

Dead leaves crunched beneath her feet.

Wildcat followed silently.

Outside, a gust of air sent Cal's brown hair into a frenzy. With her uncasted hand, she tucked a strand behind her ear, before again finding the spire's peak. It seemed to point to the heavens like a promise. She hopped onto Wildcat's boulder and opened her notebook. Wildcat leapt up next to her and began licking a paw.

With broad strokes, Cal sketched out the spire and its glowing peak, as if by copying it into her notebook she somehow made it hers. After about a half hour, Wildcat nudged her elbow. Cal scratched behind his ear. "I'm going to climb the spire and find the magic meteorite, Wildcat," she said. "I need to do it for Mom."

Wildcat purred as if saying, *Hmmmm, looks downright impossible to me.*

"I know," Cal said, lifting her chin. "But I have to." She sighed. "I'm just waiting for the right sign to tell me when."

Signs. Her mom used to be obsessed with them, back when she believed. *Whenever you have a problem—send your question into the universe, and it will answer with a sign.*

Cal often wondered if her mom put so much faith in the universe because she'd practically been on her own since her parents died when she was twelve—the same age Cal was now. *Believe in the magic of the universe,* Mom used to say.

And Cal tried to believe, even when the universe didn't seem to believe in her. Again and again, she'd sent her problems out for solving.

It doesn't work for me, she'd told her mom one afternoon in third grade. *I asked the universe why Lexi won't play with me at recess anymore, and it didn't answer with a sign or anything else.*

Maybe it did, honey. Maybe it's telling you to find a new friend. Which didn't seem like an answer at all. Cal nodded anyway, knowing that if Mom believed, that was enough for her.

Then everything turned upside down when Mom got cancer and Dad went away. Mom seemed to stop believing in signs . . . and everything else.

Cal stared hard at the spire. "Is the word in the box a sign?" she asked the mountain. "Are you leading me to the meteorite?"

The only response came from the katydids.

Again, not the answer Cal was looking for.

Wildcat leapt onto Cal's shoulder, rubbing his cheek against hers.

"I have to go, Wildcat," she said. She closed her eyes, letting his deep purr vibrate into her heart. "Please don't make it hard. You know I can't stand goodbyes." She leaned her head against his. "I'll be back tomorrow as soon as school gets out."

Wildcat blinked, then jumped back onto the boulder.

Cal scooted onto the narrow ledge. Hugging the mountain, she shimmied back across. When she reached the end, she paused, letting the cold rock press into her cheek.

"See you tomorrow," she whispered to the mountain as she patted its rough granite. Then she glanced back to give Wildcat a wave. But the boulder was bare.

Cal headed down the unmarked path until she reached the trail. When she passed the yellow sign, the sun slipped behind the mountain, bathing the world in purple twilight. A gust of wind sent leaves scurrying in a mini-tornado around her feet. She shivered.

The word. It *was* a sign. Cal was sure of it.

Now she had to figure out what it meant.

Chapter 2

Cal ran down Mountain Road, passing the Demskys' converted carriage house. Family and friends down on their luck seemed to parade through the tiny home.

Although it had sat empty for months, Cal noticed someone had opened its bright yellow curtains and a light shined in its kitchen. From the corner of her eye, she thought she saw someone watching her from the window. She slowed to double-check, but the curtain pulled shut.

Cal sped up again. She didn't know how to feel about a new neighbor. Whoever had moved in would become yet another witness to the chaos swirling around her own home.

As the sky turned darker, Cal ran faster . . . not that anyone would be looking for her. Still, *fast* was Cal's only speed.

Fast and clumsy, her classmates would say with laughter. *Cal Scott, you're as graceful as an elephant.*

She ducked and darted her way across the Demskys' yard, doing her best to avoid the elderly couple sitting on their front porch rockers. She could barely make out Mrs. Demsky's short, plump figure and Mr. Demsky's tall, skinny one. Their chairs rocked in sync—like everything else they did—as if they were one person split in two.

"Is that Calliope Scott making a ruckus?" Mr. Demsky called in his raspy voice.

Realizing the rustle of dead leaves had given her away, Cal dove behind the giant sycamore that straddled their properties. As she held her breath, the katydids' debate seemed to return full force, matching the pounding of her heart.

She didn't want the couple to see her. If they did, she'd have to acknowledge their charity and how the Demskys had basically fed them since her mom got sick and her dad went away.

"She's coming from your mountain, Father," Mrs.

Demsky said. "She goes running past this time every day."

Mr. Demsky struck a match and held it to his pipe, puffing as it lit. "From Mount Meteorite, eh?" Smoke billowed with every syllable. "Even on this bitter evening?"

"It's those stories you tell," Mrs. Demsky said. "Putting make-believe in her head—magic meteorites and the like."

"Harrumph," the old man said. "You know it's not make-believe, Mother."

Cal's ears perked at the mention of magic. It was Mr. Demsky who'd first told her about the mountain's legend.

"That girl doesn't need fantasy, Father. She needs food," Mrs. Demsky said. "Your tales of magic are fine and good, but they'd be better served with bread."

"That's your department, Mother. You brought them supper?"

"I left a pot of soup for them." Mrs. Demsky adjusted her scarf. "What else is that child going to do?" she said, waving a hand in the air. "Elaine has another treatment tomorrow. She's in no shape to cook."

Cal fumed as she listened to the couple talk about her family. *I don't need their help,* she thought, *and I sure don't need their pity.* She turned to head home, no longer caring if they heard her or not. But as she took a step, she heard a sound.

No, not a sound. A word. A song.

Then silence.

Cal froze. *Wait! What?*

The song had barely begun when it ended. Cal wasn't even sure she'd heard right. The entire song seemed to consist of a word she'd never heard before, sung over and over in a melancholy tune.

How could something so foreign seem so familiar? she wondered.

Then she knew. She hadn't *heard* the word before. She'd read it.

"What was that?" Mrs. Demsky leaned forward. The creak of her rocker paused.

"Sounds like singing. Is it coming from the Kanambes?" Mr. Demsky asked.

The couple craned their necks as if studying the carriage house and its bright kitchen light.

Still hidden behind the sycamore, Cal slipped off her backpack and dug out her notebook. She turned to the page where she'd jotted down the word that she'd found in the cave. But it was too dark to see, and she didn't want her flashlight to give her away.

"How are they settling in?" Mr. Demsky asked.

Mrs. Demsky returned to her rocking. "The young one, Rosine, seems to be doing well, but her older sister, Mali . . . I think it will take time for her."

"They're too young to be living alone," Mr. Demsky said. "I wish they'd stayed with us like we offered."

"The carriage house was empty, and they wanted their privacy. I respect that. Plus, those girls may look young, but Mali turned nineteen last week, and Rosine is wise beyond her years. I tried to bring them supper, but Rosine had already cooked. It was a simple meal, rice and beans, but she was quite happy with it."

Done with the Demskys' chatter and anxious to read the word in her notebook, Cal continued toward her house. Dead leaves crunched loudly beneath her feet.

"Who's there?" Mrs. Demsky called out, leaning forward. "Sounds like a bear!"

Cal leapt back to the safety of her sycamore.

Mr. Demsky kept rocking. "No bears today. It's only the leaves you hear. They're so dry, they'll make a cricket sound like an elephant." He blew pipe smoke in a perfect circle. Cal watched it glide upward. "So, tell me, Mother, what makes you think there isn't magic on our mountain?"

The old woman laid her wrinkled hand across her

husband's. "Your stories aren't going to help Calliope Scott right now." Mrs. Demsky seemed to study her husband. "I know that look, Father. What mischief are you up to?"

"No mischief." The old man nodded. "It's just time."

"Time for what?"

"If you ask those crickets, they'll tell you it's time for winter. Listen how loudly they sing! *Look at me!* they're saying. *I have a lot to tell you and little time left!*"

"Is that what they're saying, Father?"

"It's what we're all saying, Mother."

"Ha!" Mrs. Demsky leaned forward in her chair. "Cricket or bear or elephant, our mountain has turned out its light, and so must I." She awkwardly hoisted herself from the chair with a grunt. "And you need to stop smoking that pipe and take your medicine."

Mr. Demsky coughed. "Another minute for me, Mother. I want to say good night to the critters."

Mrs. Demsky sighed. "I'll put the kettle on. Don't be long."

As the front door opened, the yellow warmth of their home seemed to pour out like maple syrup. Cal watched Mr. Demsky pull his collar tight against the night.

"On Mount Meteorite . . . ," he began, even though his wife had left.

The katydids' chatter turned silent, as if they were holding on to each word.

"On Mount Meteorite," he repeated, "there are no stories. There is only magic."

Right then, the word popped back into Cal's head.

The word she'd just heard.

"Amani!" she said, before slapping her good hand across her mouth.

The old man laughed.

Cal darted off.

She didn't care that she sounded like a herd of elephants. She needed to see that word again.

Chapter 3

When Cal reached her front steps, she found the soup pot Mrs. Demsky had left. She picked it up and went inside. The soup was still warm.

Without turning on a light, she set the pot on the kitchen table. Using her flashlight to see, she leafed through her notebook until she found the word.

"Amani," she whispered. "I *was* right." Cal smiled an inside smile. It was a habit she'd learned years ago to hide her emotions. It seemed that any time she was brave enough to share an outside smile with the world, someone or something would show up to snatch her happiness away.

"But what does *amani* mean?"

There was a time when Cal would have immediately fired up her laptop to search for the word, but the Scotts hadn't had Wi-Fi since her dad lost his job.

She had another idea. She walked over to the wooden desk in the corner. She moved aside a broken picture frame and began sorting through unpaid bills until she found her mom's old dictionary.

She flipped through the *A*'s until she got to the page that began with *alyssum* and ended with *ambiversive*. Her finger traced the left column until she came to *amalgamation*—the process of being amalgamated. Then she came to *amanita*—any of various mostly poisonous white-spored fungi.

No *amani*.

"Cal?"

She turned toward the dark family room to find her mother lying on the couch.

Mom sat up. "What time is it? What are you doing?"

Cal shut the dictionary and hustled back to the table. She returned her notebook to her backpack. "I thought you were in bed," she said. "I didn't mean to wake you."

Mom walked shakily into the kitchen and flicked on the light. "No, it's okay. I was waiting for you." She fell into a chair.

Cal blinked hard. She preferred the darkness. If she couldn't see, she couldn't be reminded of things.

Missing things.

Like the way her father wasn't at the stove whipping up his famous grilled cheese.

And broken things.

Like the fist-size hole in the wall.

As much as she tried to avoid it, the hole was like a magnet for her eyes, and she found herself, once again, staring into its empty space.

Mom noticed. "I'm sorry I haven't fixed that yet," she said, waving a hand in the air.

The truth was her mother had tried. She'd hung a picture of the three of them hiking Tuckerman's Ravine over the hole. But when the frame fell and its glass shattered, Mom had stopped trying. Now the broken frame, and its family, lay discarded among the piles of bills littering the desk.

"Homemade chicken soup," Mom said as she removed the lid. "Mrs. Demsky is so thoughtful. I told her how good her soup felt after my last treatment. Can you grab some bowls, honey?"

Cal retrieved dishes and silverware from the cupboard and ladled the soup. As she handed a bowl to her mother, she made sure to avoid eye contact. It was something she'd started doing soon after Mom began chemo. Cal felt that if their eyes met, she'd have to acknowledge the truth. Her mother had changed. Not all at once, but little by little.

At first it was the way her mother was always tired. She remembered coming home from school on a sunny May afternoon to find Mom asleep in bed. "Sorry, I needed to lie down for a sec. I'm good now," her mother had said. But then it happened again and again, and Cal learned that spending time on the mountain with Wildcat was easier than watching Mom pretend she wasn't tired.

Then there were the big clumps of Mom's brown curls in the trash. When Cal asked about them, Mom had said that when the chemo killed cancer cells, it killed her hair cells too. It wasn't long before she was completely bald. She'd even lost her eyebrows and eyelashes. She didn't even smell like Mom anymore.

But the biggest change was how fragile Mom had become. Her soft squishiness had turned into hard edges hidden beneath baggy clothes. Most of the time Cal was scared to even touch her mother, never mind hug her. She was pretty sure that no matter how careful she was, Mom would break.

"I don't want you going up on that mountain anymore," Mom said, interrupting her thoughts. "It gets dark so early now. And cold."

Cal nodded, but she knew her mother wouldn't do anything to stop her.

Mom took a sip of broth. "Thanks, Cal. This is exactly what I needed."

Cal smiled on the inside. She was glad to see Mom eat.

"So, what do you do on that mountain all alone?" Mom said.

Cal wanted to tell her that she wasn't alone. The mountain was her friend—more than any friend she'd ever had at school. She wanted to say, *Telling me I can't go on the mountain is like telling me I can't breathe.* Instead, she said, "I'm not alone. Wildcat is with me."

"A stray," Mom said, taking another sip, "that's full of fleas and ticks and probably rabies. That makes me feel better."

"Wildcat doesn't have any of those. Plus, we have plenty to do. We're going to find the magic meteorite."

"Calliope Scott, you are twelve years old and too old to believe in fairy tales," her mother said.

"You used to believe it," Cal said. "You used to tell me the magic meteorite story at bedtime."

"Dad told you that story, not me. It was a local legend told to little kids for fun. When you grow up, you find out there's no such thing as magic."

"Well, how do you explain the green light people

saw streak across the sky and land on the spire? Once, Mr. Demsky told me about how he actually saw it happen."

"That story's been around longer than I have." Mom shook her head. "And seems to have grown bigger and bigger over the years. I doubt any of it really happened, but even if it did, I'm sure there's a perfectly good explanation." She sighed. "I know Mr. Demsky loves to weave his tales of magic, but enough. Okay, Cal? We need to be grown-ups now. Both of us."

Cal stared at her own soup.

"And speaking of acting grown-up . . ." Mom tugged at her right earlobe, the way she always did when she was nervous or upset. "I need you to come straight home after school Friday."

"Why?"

"We are going to visit Dad."

Cal shook her head. "No way."

"He's been at Davison Correctional for over a month, and you haven't gone to see him once. This whole thing is eating him up. He needs to see you, Cal." Her mother sighed. "And you need to see him."

A piece of celery stuck to the back of Cal's throat. She coughed. Then coughed again.

"Are you okay?" Mom asked.

Cal stumbled to the sink and drank straight from the tap. She wiped her mouth before spinning around. Then she focused her gaze on the black hole in the wall.

"I'm. Not. Going," she said.

"Cal . . . ," her mother began.

Without another word, Cal snatched up her backpack and darted to her room. She closed the door and leaned against it, remembering the hurt and pain from the night the black hole happened.

The tears came, then. Hot and fast.

When someone keeps a secret, it either means they don't trust you or that they're too ashamed to accept the truth.

For Cal, the black hole was full of secrets.

She walked over to her window and stared at the mountain. Even though it was barely visible against the night, she felt it watching and waiting for her to return. She sat on her bed and pulled out her notebook, then opened it to her map and silently traced the path she'd marked to get to the spire. Over and over and over, like a prayer.

After a while, her eyelids began to feel heavy, but Cal wouldn't give in to sleep. She couldn't. Because as much as the mountain looked out for her during the day, it couldn't protect her from the night.

Cal stood and began pacing.

Around and around the edges of her braided rug, she walked in a tight circle, cradling her casted arm. Around and around until finally, for just a millisecond, she lay across her bed to rest her eyes.

That's when she fell into the darkness of sleep. Slipping away from the mountain. Away from its magic.

The nightmare was always the same.

Cal is standing in front of the black hole. She begins to peer into it when all of a sudden, she's sucked inside, then pulled down a long dark tunnel.

When it ends, she finds herself standing at the end of a narrow hallway. It's so white and polished and shiny it makes her eyes sting.

There are doors on either side of the hallway—one after the other. She tries to yank the first one open, but it's locked. She tries another and another . . . but she can't get inside any of them.

She squints, peering down the length of the corridor. There is a large mirror at the very end.

Without taking a step, her body begins to move forward, toward the mirror, as if caught in a river's current.

But there's no water.

She rotates her arms backward, trying to stop, but

instead she's pulled faster and faster, zooming toward the mirror until she is standing right in front of it.

She looks into it and sees an unearthly white face staring back. But it's not really staring, because where its eyes should be are empty black sockets.

"Who are you?" Cal demands.

Gray vapor pours from the empty eyes.

Cal opens her mouth to scream, but no sound comes out. She tries to turn, to run, but she can't move.

The vapor crawls over her skin and enters her veins—it's an instant coldness, like falling into a frozen lake.

The mirror-person opens its mouth to talk, but Cal can't hear anything. She flaps her arms wildly. A scream lodges in her throat. She tries again and again until she finally coughs out a word.

"NO!"

Cal blinked her eyes open. She was back in her dark bedroom. The hallway and its doors and mirror and angry, empty eye sockets were gone.

She took a deep breath, then crawled under the covers. She peered out her dark window, finding Mount Meteorite's giant profile. For the rest of the night, Cal kept her gaze fixed on it, as if it were a shelter in the midst of a wild storm.

Chapter 4

At 7 A.M., Cal turned off the alarm before it had time to buzz. She rolled to the edge of her bed. When her feet hit the ground, she hugged herself, doing her best to shiver away the night.

At her closet, she studied the few shirts and pants hanging there. She put on a T-shirt, wondering if it had shrunk. No one had taken her back-to-school shopping, and it seemed most of her clothes were too small, especially with the cast. She turned away from the empty hangers and instead dug through her backpack for her newest find—a soft pink sweatshirt. She slipped it over the T-shirt, letting the sleeve where her left arm belonged dangle loose and empty. Even though it wasn't a good color, like green or brown, it was warm and soft, and the sleeves reached her wrist.

When she had first woken up from her nightmare, she'd lain in bed listening to the creak of floorboards as her mother made her way back to the couch. She knew it meant that Mom couldn't sleep again and had probably returned to the family room to watch TV.

Now, as Cal tiptoed through the kitchen and into the family room, she could see her mother still there, wrapped in a blanket and sound asleep. The morning news droned in the background.

The soft cap Mom wore at home had slipped off, revealing her bald head. Cal willed her to wake up and be the mom she used to know. The one who made hot buttered toast for breakfast and packed cucumber sandwiches in a chilled lunchbox.

Without notice, Cal's mind flashed back to the first time she met this new, tired mom.

It was May. Cal was still in sixth grade and had been working on her science project. The assignment was to re-create any element from the periodic table. Most kids used jelly beans or gummies, but Cal wanted her element to be extra scientific and serious. She also wanted it to be difficult. So she chose a radioactive, artificially produced element called oganesson. She had it all planned: She'd use clothes hangers to show its seven electron orbitals, and wooden beads to represent its electrons, neutrons, and protons.

The good part was that oganesson had the highest atomic number. The bad part was that she would need 412 beads.

"Mom, can you take me to CraftCart? Now?" she'd asked.

Mom sat slumped at the desk, sorting bills. "Now? Can't you wait for Dad?"

"It will be closed then. Please! I need one hundred and twelve more beads to make my element."

"What about switching to something easier? How about helium?"

"Helium has an atomic number of two. Two protons, two neutrons, two electrons, and one orbital. It would be completely boring!"

Mom sighed. "Okay, fine. Let's go."

Inside CraftCart, Cal tugged on her mother's arm. "Why are you walking so slow?"

"Isn't there anywhere to sit?" Mom asked.

"I'm almost done. I need to grab some more sticks for the glue gun."

"I'll wait here," Mom said, leaning against a shelf filled with colorful yarn.

When Cal got back, her mother was sitting on the floor.

"What are you doing?" Cal asked. She tugged on her mother's arm to get up.

"I'm sorry. I had to sit for a minute."

"On the ground?"

"Okay, relax. I'm up. Let's go."

Cal studied her mom. Then the beads in her cart. "I'm sorry, Mom. I—"

"It's fine. Ready?"

When they got home, Dad was boiling water for pasta.

"Thanks, honey," Mom said as she curled up on the couch.

Cal went to work at the kitchen table. "Mom?" she called. "Can you hold the clothes hanger while I glue the beads in place?"

When her mother didn't answer, Cal peeked into the family room. Mom was snoring.

Cal stared at her half-finished oganesson. Suddenly, she didn't feel like making the hardest element anymore. She went into her room and tossed it in the trash.

Then she started making helium.

Mom shifted on the couch, and her cap fell to the floor. Cal picked it up and placed it by her hand. Then pulled the blanket to her mother's chin.

Before that day at CraftCart, Cal had thought her Mom would be better soon. But here they were, five months later. Mom was still tired, and Cal was still tip-toeing around her.

Cal flicked the television off and went into the kitchen. She grabbed a granola bar and filled her water bottle.

At the front door, she slipped into her hiking boots without lacing them. She slung her backpack across her shoulder and ducked outside.

The frosty morning air blew away any remaining sleep-cobwebs, and Cal began to run.

Halfway down Mountain Road, she could see the distant headlights of the school bus as it made its way along Main Street.

It was a race now. Who would make it to the bus stop first? Cal's boots slapped the ground as adrenaline pumped through her body.

On the corner, Demsky's Market glowed like a beacon against the dark morning. Cal ran toward it as the bus's lights blinked yellow, then red, and its door slowly folded open.

For as long as she could remember, Cal was the only one getting on at that stop. However, on that morning, a new girl stood on the curb. In the nick of time, Cal pivoted, barely missing her before pounding up the steps and sliding into the first empty seat.

"You must be the new one," the driver said to the kid who hadn't budged from the curb. "Come on, now. I've got a schedule to keep."

Soft footsteps made their way up until a petite girl wearing an oversize green hoodie, jeans, and sandals stood at the front of the bus and peered into its dark aisle.

The bus lurched forward, and the girl fell into the seat with Cal, who immediately scooted as far as she could against the cold metal wall. Soon Cal's knees began to bounce as if they needed to keep moving, even though there was nowhere to go. She knew this made an annoying thumping sound on the hollow floor, but she couldn't help it.

The new girl didn't seem to notice, or mind anyway. She sat rigidly hugging a purple backpack. Cal wondered if this girl was the person she'd seen behind the yellow curtain at the Demskys' carriage house.

As the bus stopped for more kids, Cal glanced at the new girl. Her skin was dark brown, and her black hair was cut in short, tight curls. She seemed to be clenching her teeth as if trying to stop them from chattering, but every now and then they'd start again. Something about it—the clenching, the chattering—made Cal's jaw hurt.

They continued down Main to School Street, eventually pulling into the bus line. As the doors folded open, Cal waited for the girl to stand up so they could get off. But she stayed seated, letting everyone else go first. When the bus was empty, Cal followed her before heading into the swarm of students. From the corner of her eye, she saw the girl pause as if deciding whether she was going to join them.

For a millisecond, Cal considered asking her if she needed help, then shook her head. *No way*, she thought. She wasn't going to let this girl suck her in like the others had. She'd been friends with another "new girl" briefly in third grade. But as soon as Tonia Applebee learned her way around school, it seemed she'd also learned to stay away from "weird" Cal Scott. It had been a hard lesson, but one Cal wouldn't forget: *If you don't have friends, then no one can hurt you.*

Cal didn't bother with a locker. She kept her backpack on at all times. It was useful if she needed to make a clean escape or tuck away an item she might need later.

In the hallway, Cal scanned the lost-and-found table, making a mental note of what was there. Most items were still warm-weather gear. She could see a left-footed cleat, a mud-soaked sock, sports pinnies, water bottles, and baseball caps. Even though mornings hadn't been cold enough for a lost winter coat or boots, it was never too early to look. After all, she'd already found the sweat-shirt there.

Fortunately, homeroom was also science, Cal's favor-ite class. But even science couldn't protect her from Lexi and Tonia. She referred to them as the Bee Girls for the way they swarmed and buzzed around her, tossing insults.

Cal took her seat as the first bell rang. The Bee Girls hovered like a wasps' nest about to fall.

Cal's knees bounced.

Ignore those girls, she reminded herself as she dug out her notebook. Unfortunately, that only seemed to make the buzzing turn louder with words that vibrated straight into her skin—*thief, liar, pathetic.*

In moments like this, Cal had learned to close her eyes and imagine she was on Mount Meteorite, hik-ing a trail with Wildcat, collecting birch bark to build a fire, or finding blackberries to snack on back at the cave.

There was a tap on her shoulder.

When Cal was small, she rarely got angry. But ever since *the day when everything changed*, things that used to make her sad or frustrated or disappointed now made her angry. All it took was a small flicker to ignite what felt like a red, hot ember deep inside her core. Once that ember lit, there was no putting it out.

Right then, Tonia's tap on her shoulder was enough to spark the flame.

Cal spun toward the Bee Girls. "Don't. Touch. Me!"

Tonia Applebee stood with a quivering lip. Behind her, Lexi pretended to study the dyed pink ends of her own long blond hair.

"Say it." Lexi nudged Tonia.

Tonia looked at her feet. "Th-that's Lexi's Glō sweatshirt you're wearing," she mumbled.

"No, it's not," Cal said.

Another shove by Lexi.

"Lexi knows it's hers," Tonia continued, "because it's Glō and because there's a purple nail polish stain on the elbow that she got when she was getting ready for spirit day." She started to point at the stain, but then seemed to change her mind and crossed her arms.

Cal glanced at the sleeve. *Careless!* she thought. She usually made sure there were no telltale marks. She shook her head. "That's from the purple nail polish I always use."

The buzz of the Bee Girls got louder.

"Let's see your hands," Lexi said. "I don't see any nail polish."

"I took it off this morning."

Lexi pushed Tonia out of the way. "You're such a liar, Cal. That's my sweatshirt, and you know it."

"Prove it," Cal sneered.

Lexi's mouth dropped open. "You can't make me," she said, but her forehead wrinkled as if she was worried she really might have to.

"We all know *your* parents don't buy Glō," Tonia said with a smirk.

"Yeah." Lexi grinned. "I don't think they sell Glō in jail."

Cal blinked hard, trying to pretend she hadn't just gotten stung. As she turned away, she noticed the new girl from the bus standing outside the classroom, hugging her purple backpack.

"Ladies, what's going on here?" Mr. Lopez was suddenly in front of Cal. He didn't seem to notice the lost-looking girl in the doorway watching them.

"Cal stole Lexi's sweatshirt, and now she won't give it back," Tonia said.

Lexi nodded furiously.

Mr. Lopez's thick gray eyebrows arched. Even though he was one of the oldest teachers in school, he acted like one of the youngest and usually knew how to talk to kids in a way that showed he cared. But right then, as his gaze shifted between Tonia and Lexi, he didn't seem to know what to do with the Bee Girls' accusation. Cal could tell by the way he hugged his waist with his left hand and pinched his chin with his right. It was something he always did when deep in thought.

Tonia grabbed Cal's sleeve to show the stain to Mr. Lopez. "See! Lexi's nail polish!"

Lexi wiggled her fingers to prove it.

Cal jerked the sleeve back. "I said, don't *touch* me!" She narrowed her eyes, wishing she could shoot laser beams from them. She'd disintegrate Lexi Nesbitt in two blinks.

The Bee Girls took a step back, their buzzing temporarily silenced.

The second bell rang.

"Lots of people have pink sweatshirts, Lexi," Mr. Lopez said. "Let's not jump to conclusions."

"But it's Glō," Lexi whined. "And it has nail—"

"Take your seat, Lexi."

As Lexi stomped off, Mr. Lopez leaned on Cal's desk. "Hey, Scott, how's your dad?" he whispered. Mr. Lopez was part of her father's rock climbing community. He had known Cal since she was little and had a habit of calling her by her last name.

Cal's cheeks burned. If there had been a way for her to crawl inside her desk right then, she would have. "Mr. Lopez, can you call me Cal in school?" she whispered.

"Right, you've told me that." He nodded slowly. "When you talk to your dad, let him know that I'm thinking of him, okay?" Mr. Lopez said. "I'm planning to visit him again this weekend."

Cal stared at her desk. Did he really have to bring Dad up in school where other kids might hear? Without answering, she slipped lower in her seat.

"Let me know if your mom needs anything." Mr. Lopez gave Cal's desk a pat before making his way to the front of the classroom. Halfway there, he seemed to notice the new girl standing in the doorway.

"Aha!" he said. "Rosine Kanambe, I presume?"

The girl nodded.

He walked toward her. "Welcome, welcome, I heard I might be getting a new student today." He reached out to give her a fist bump.

When she only stared back, he shoved his hands in his pockets.

"Well, come on in. There's a spot next to Sc—I mean, Cal." He nodded toward the empty desk before continuing to the front.

Rosine tiptoed over and slid into the chair.

"Well done." Mr. Lopez pinched his chin. "We're all here. Let's begin."

Chapter 5

"Today, we continue our earth science unit investigating how mountains are formed," Mr. Lopez said as an image of Mount Meteorite flashed across the SMART board.

Cal sat up. If Mr. Lopez had simply opened the blinds, they could see the real Mount Meteorite through the window. Instead, they stared at a grainy black-and-white image that looked as if it had been taken one hundred years ago.

"We're lucky here in Bleakerville to have our own mountain, albeit a small one," Mr. Lopez continued as he waved around the yardstick he used as a pointer. "Can anyone tell me how Mount Meteorite was formed?"

Hands shot up.

"Luis?" he said, pointing the yardstick at a kid in the back.

"A magical meteorite landed there."

A smile almost crept across Cal's face, but she bit her lip to stop it. Luis Baez had only moved to town last month, but he'd clearly already been schooled on the local town legend.

Mr. Lopez closed his eyes for a moment. Then opened them. "Friends," he began slowly. "This is science class, and you are seventh graders." His bushy gray eyebrows arched. "As I've told you before, science derives from fact. Not fiction."

Cal knew what was coming next. When Mr. Lopez got wound up on a topic, he used his yardstick pointer for emphasis. Kind of like a loud exclamation point. The entire class held their breath. Cal braced for impact.

"Fact!" Mr. Lopez slapped the yardstick on the front table with a loud *thwhack!* Luis jumped in his seat. "Fifty years ago, people claimed they saw a bright green light streak across the sky and land on Bleaker Mountain's spire."

"Bleaker Mountain?" Luis said. "You mean Mount Meteorite."

"Fact!" Mr. Lopez exclaimed. "At that time, it was called Bleaker Mountain."

The new girl had taken out a notebook and was writing every word down. Cal rolled her eyes.

"From this alleged spectacle, a *magical* meteorite was purportedly deposited on the mountain's spire." He wiggled his fingers when he said *magical*.

Kids laughed.

Luis's cheeks turned pink.

"Fact! Based on this illogical and scientifically absurd legend, the name of the mountain was changed to Mount Meteorite. However," he continued, "no one has ever found said meteorite, and there's no evidence there really was a green flash or that it came from a meteor in the first place."

Rosine raised her hand. "I don't know this word, *meteorite*," she said. "Please tell me what it is?"

Along with everyone else in class, Cal turned to stare at the new girl. The way she emphasized her syllables differently—pronouncing MEE-tee-yor-ite, like mee-TYOR-ite—made it clear that she wasn't from anywhere near Bleakerville. But even more surprising was the way she'd asked the question so boldly. Cal was embarrassed to admit when she didn't understand something at school—a math problem or a new vocabulary word. But not this girl. Even her tone seemed to demand the answer.

"Ahh! Good question. What is a meteorite?" Mr. Lopez

wrapped his left arm across his waist, pinching his chin with his right. "Cal, you look like you have something to say."

Cal flinched. She knew that talking in class made her an even bigger target for the Bee Girls. But she wasn't going to let them, or anyone else, silence her when it came to science. She took a deep breath.

"It's a rock from space that's crashed to earth," she said.

As if on cue, the Bee Girls' buzzing got louder. Cal couldn't tell if Mr. Lopez didn't hear or was just ignoring them.

"Well, yes, that," Mr. Lopez said. "When a piece of space debris, called a meteoroid, falls through the atmosphere, the resistance from the air makes it extremely hot. The fireball or 'shooting star' you see is the meteor. And if the meteor survives that trip and hits the earth, it's called a meteorite."

Cal racked her brain as she thought back to her fifth-grade unit on space. "When the rock is still in space, it's called a meteoroid," she said. "When it enters our atmosphere, it's called a meteor. And when it hits the ground, it's called a meteorite. Right?"

Mr. Lopez slapped the front table with his yardstick. "Fact!" he exclaimed.

Cal smiled on the inside.

"But we are not doing our space unit today," Mr. Lopez said. "We are talking about mountains and the various ways they are formed, including by plate tectonics and volcanic eruption," he continued. "Mount Meteorite is a pegmatite. It formed through igneous intrusion when molten rock erupted through the earth's crust." He pointed his yardstick at the image of the mountain still projected across the SMART board. "Erosion from wind, snow, and rain caused softer rock to wear away. Leaving behind the one-hundred-foot-tall chimney-like spire that forms its peak."

Like her bouncing knees, Cal's mouth had a mind of its own, and sometimes she couldn't stop herself from talking, especially when it had to do with the mountain and its magic.

"But . . . the meteorite . . . ," she blurted out. "The one that people say landed on top of that spire . . . just because no one's found it doesn't mean it isn't there, right? If it is, how do we know it isn't magical?"

This time the entire class turned to stare at Cal. But even that didn't stop her words from spilling out. "Because . . . there was that green streak of light people saw . . . and, you know, well . . . I know someone who saw it for real." Cal was starting to feel dizzy. She took a deep breath. "Even though no one's ever found the meteorite, couldn't the legend be, like, a hypothesis that hasn't been proven yet?"

"And what about the scientists?" Luis jumped in. "I heard two scientists scaled the spire looking for the meteorite. What did they find?"

Mr. Lopez walked briskly toward the blinds and opened them, revealing the real Mount Meteorite.

"Fact," Mr. Lopez said. "There were two geologists from the university who climbed the spire to look for the meteorite people *claimed* they saw land there."

He turned to face the class. "*Claimed*," he repeated. "Not proved."

"But what *did* they see?" Luis asked, almost falling out of his seat.

"No one knows, because no one ever heard from them again," he said quietly. "And that's a fact." He turned back to the image of the mountain, hugging his waist with his left arm while pinching his chin with his right.

It was part of the legend that Cal knew well. Everyone in town had gathered to watch the geologists head up the mountain; no one ever saw them come down. It was as if they'd disappeared into thin air.

"Those scientists died," Lexi said. "That's what my grandpa told me. He said they fell and died and their bodies landed where no one could find them."

Other kids began nodding as if they'd heard the same story.

"Yeah," Tonia said. "My cousin and his friend tried to climb the spire, but they barely got off the ground. They said it's smooth as glass. Totally impossible."

"Did anyone look for the scientists?" Luis asked. "Someone must have found something."

Every eye was on Mr. Lopez, but his gaze remained fixed on the grainy photo.

"There is a great deal of mystery swirling about Mount Meteorite," he finally said. "Stories about what those geologists found . . . and what they didn't." His voice seemed to dissolve to a whisper. "But that's all they are. Stories," he said. "Fiction." He cleared his throat. "Let's get back to science, shall we?"

He pressed the remote, and a new mountain appeared on the screen. "Now, here is Mount Whitney in California. Whitney and the Sierra Nevada are a fault-block range. Block mountains can be formed in two ways. First, when . . ."

Mr. Lopez kept talking, but Cal wasn't listening. She stared at Mount Meteorite, wishing she could jump out the window and run there. Soon her knees began to bounce all over again.

As class droned on, the walls of the classroom seemed

to shrink. Cal wanted to be ready to escape as soon as the bell rang. She turned to gaze out the open door. As she did, her eyes met Rosine's. The new girl was smiling at her so eagerly Cal could almost hear a question in it.

Do not smile back! Cal chided herself.

By the time the bell announced the end of science, Cal was ready to dash. The way Rosine kept staring at her every time Mr. Lopez paused, she could tell the girl was trying to talk to her or, worse, become friends. But all Cal cared about was disappearing herself quickly, before the Bee Girls could start up that business about the sweatshirt again.

Down the hall she raced, before ducking into the girls' lavatory. With her good hand, she ripped off the sweatshirt. She tugged down her too-small T-shirt, then bolted back out. As she strolled by the lost-and-found table, she tossed the sweatshirt on the pile and kept going. Before she turned the corner, she paused to see if Lexi and Tonia had noticed it.

Instead, there was Rosine.

Again.

Cal watched her walk up to the table and pick up the sweatshirt.

"Lexi!" Tonia rushed up and grabbed it from Rosine's hand. "I found it! She must have put it back."

Lexi took the sweatshirt from Tonia and made a face. She returned it to the pile.

"What are you doing?" Tonia asked.

"I don't want it." Lexi looked at her outstretched fingers. "The nail polish ruined it. I just didn't want Cal Scott to have it."

"Oh." Tonia frowned.

"Can I have it?" Rosine asked.

Tonia's forehead seemed to wrinkle in confusion.

"I mean, if you don't want it. It looks warm, and . . ." Rosine's words fell away.

The Bees tilted their heads in unison.

Lexi scanned the new girl up and down in a way that made Cal want to run off again. But something about the way Rosine raised her chin as she met their stares made her stay.

"Whatever, I don't care," Lexi said coolly. "Come on, Tonia."

As the Bee Girls sauntered off, Rosine stuffed the sweatshirt inside her purple backpack.

Of course, Cal thought as she made her way to math. *It can be for anyone as long as that anyone isn't Cal Scott.*

Chapter 6

Over the summer when Cal had been exploring the mountain, she came across a silver maple tree. She could immediately see it was the perfect spot to rest and climb. Something about its armlike branches felt like a hug.

Then one day, after a windstorm, she found the tree on its side. Its limbs seemed to reach upward as if begging for help. When she examined its trunk, she realized that despite its dark green leaves and rugged bark, a fungus had invaded it, eating the tree from the inside out and leaving it hollow. All those days it had appeared fine on the outside, it was really dying on the inside.

When Cal was at school, she felt like that hollow silver maple.

I'll be on the mountain soon, she reminded herself as she ran toward the afternoon bus. That thought was almost enough to make her smile—on the inside, anyway.

She hopped onto the bus, expecting to sit in her usual seat, but Rosine was already sitting there. She looked up at Cal and grinned before adjusting her purple backpack as if to make room.

For a millisecond, Cal considered the offer. Then she remembered the scene at the lost-and-found table. Maybe Rosine had asked the Bee Girls for the pink sweatshirt because she wanted to be friends with them. Maybe she was exactly like them. Cal narrowed her eyes at the new girl before moving on to find an empty seat.

Fortunately, her stop was close. But, as anxious as Cal was to get to the mountain, she needed something first.

When the bus chugged to a stop, she leapt from its top step as usual, but instead of darting up Mountain Road, she dashed up the front steps of Demsky's Market.

Inside, the bell dinged. She scanned the shop, taking in its wide, worn floorboards and half-empty shelves. The windows were stained with the grime of so many winters that any dust-filled light that was able to fight its way inside appeared dull and gray.

Cal sneezed.

Her plan was to get what she needed—quick—and

51

get out before anyone saw her. Hopefully, Mr. Demsky would be tucked in his back office as usual.

"Hello there, Calliope Scott."

It was the Misses—Miss McAllister and Miss Bamina. Two elderly ladies from her mother's quilting group. Even though they were inseparable, they looked and dressed completely opposite of each other.

Tall and skinny Miss McAllister was pale and freckled. She wore long sleeves and pants, even in summer, and never stopped wearing a face mask even though the pandemic had ended.

Shorter and thicker Miss Bamina had brown skin and wore a new hair color each time Cal saw her—red, pink, even orange once. As usual, she was dressed in sporty sneakers and tights as if she were about to run a marathon.

"How's Mom, Calliope?" Miss Bamina asked as she handed Miss McAllister a jar of preserved peaches.

"Fine," Cal said. She was curious why they were putting food on the shelves instead of in their cart, but she didn't have time to ask.

"Please give her our regards." Miss Bamina winked. "And let her know we'll be by later this week to drop off a basket the Quilt Crew put together for her."

Miss McAllister nodded, but because of her mask, Cal couldn't tell if she was happy about that or not. The ladies returned to their shelving.

Cal took the opportunity to duck into the aisle marked CANNED MEAT & FISH. As she did, she noticed that Rosine was still outside, staring at the market.

"Can I help you find something?" Tall, pimply Abner Dunlop stood at the end of the aisle, arms crossed. He wore a long white apron around his waist and a sarcastic grin on his face.

Cal sighed. Abner would complicate things.

"Abner, honey, we're leaving! Can you help us carry these boxes out?" Miss Bamina called.

He narrowed his eyes as he walked past Cal.

She breathed a sigh of relief, then scanned the shelves, quickly finding what she'd come for. She snatched up the small yellow tin of sardines as if it were a piece of gold.

Of course, she didn't have any money to pay for it, but she'd heard Mr. Demsky tell her mother that they were welcome to take anything they needed from the market. That probably meant they were supposed to *ask* first, but Mom would never ask for this, and Cal was too embarrassed.

She shoved the can inside the sling of her cast.

Suddenly the front door dinged again. Abner must have returned, because she could hear him greet a new customer with his "Can I help you find something?"

Good, she thought, *that will keep him busy.* She picked up another can and then another, shoving them inside the open space of her sling, one at a time. She wondered how many would fit.

"What are you doing?"

Cal spun to see Rosine staring at her. At first, Cal was confused.

Then she was angry.

"Stop following me!" Cal shouted. But as she turned to leave, there was Abner again. Standing behind Rosine.

"What's going on here?" he demanded.

Cal pushed past them and darted out the front door. The bell dinged loudly as she leapt over the steps and onto the pavement. She wasn't sure if Abner had seen what she'd taken, but she was pretty sure Rosine would tell him.

She didn't have time to worry about that now. She glanced at the spire's peak, already ignited. She needed to get to the cave and Wildcat before the sun dipped any lower.

"Hey! Stop!" a voice called out.

Against her better judgment, Cal turned.

Rosine pulled something pink from her backpack and waved it at Cal. "I got this for you!" she shouted.

Cal squinted. Clutched tight in Rosine's fist was Lexi's Glō sweatshirt.

What?

Right then, Abner came rolling toward Cal like a runaway grocery cart on a windy day.

"Not so fast!" he shouted before grabbing her arm.

Cal's mouth fell open. Her gaze darted between Abner and Rosine. *It was a setup!* She tried to break free, but Abner had a tight grip on her. He twisted her good arm behind her back.

"Ow!" Cal screamed.

"Think you're so smart now?" he asked.

"Hey!" Rosine shouted. "Stop! You're hurting her!"

"You her accomplice?" Abner asked Rosine as he dragged Cal into the store. After they'd tumbled back inside, he called out, "Mr. Demsky!"

"Let go of me!" Cal said. "I didn't do anything."

"Oh yeah?" Abner dug his hand into the sling and held up one of the yellow tins. "Sardines? Seriously?"

"Now, now, what's this ruckus about?" Mr. Demsky stood near the front counter, one hand gripping his cane, the other, his left suspender. He wore a blue flannel shirt that had a hole in the elbow, baggy pants, and a long white apron like Abner's. With watery black eyes, he looked at them. One. At. A. Time.

"I caught these two shoplifting, Mr. Demsky." Abner held up the tin.

Cal glanced sideways at Rosine. "I don't even know her. And I wasn't stealing . . . I was . . . Well, I heard you tell my mom we could . . ." Her gaze fell to the floor.

Mr. Demsky collected the tin from Abner. Then he coughed into his handkerchief.

"Why don't you ladies come to my office?" he said in his gravelly voice.

"Should I call the police, Mr. Demsky?" Abner took a step toward an old-fashioned phone.

"I don't think they're *too* dangerous, but thank you, Abner." Mr. Demsky winked. "Mrs. Schirra dropped off some canned tomatoes earlier, and Lopez brought over a case of paper towels. You can put those things out for our shoppers." Mr. Demsky headed toward the back of the store.

"Rosine shouldn't have to stay," Cal said. "She didn't have anything to do with it." She felt bad for dragging the new girl into this situation, but mostly she was worried Rosine would whisper her business back to the Bee Girls.

If they found out she'd been caught shoplifting, soon the entire school would know.

Without turning, Mr. Demsky chuckled. "Maybe not that. But she has plenty to do with everything else. Come with me, ladies. Let's chat in my office. Everything is as it should be."

Chapter 7

The small room at the back of the store looked more like a science lab than the office of a food market. Instead of papers, Mr. Demsky's desk was littered with rocks. A small table held a microscope surrounded by more stone fragments. A giant bookshelf reached the ceiling and was crammed with books in faded greens and browns. Posters of rocks papered the walls. Cal recognized some from the mountain—shiny black isinglass, clear crystal quartz, pinkish rhodonite.

A long table was cluttered with photos. Some were framed, and some loose. Cal knew that when he was younger, Mr. Demsky had been part of her dad's climbing community, so she wasn't surprised to see that most of the pictures were of men and women on mountains wearing T-shirts with the Ragged Mountain Climbers Club logo.

Cal studied the photos, wondering if there was a picture of her dad buried among them. She picked up a grainy black-and-white photo of two young men wearing baggy pants. Climbing ropes were slung across their shoulders. They stood on a tall peak next to a milk-white boulder. Even though Cal didn't know them, there was something in their eyes that she recognized. A feeling, really. One she experienced each time she was on the mountain.

"Don't mind the mess," Mr. Demsky said as he fell into a chair. "Have a seat, ladies. You must be hungry coming from school. Let me see what I have here." He dug inside a drawer and lifted out an opened package of gingersnaps.

Cal put the photo down and sat. Even though her stomach rumbled with hunger, she didn't feel comfortable accepting Mr. Demsky's generosity after what she'd done. She shook her head.

"No, thank you," Rosine said in a small voice.

"Really?" Mr. Demsky dug his hand inside the bag. "Well, then I'll have to eat yours." He paused. "Our secret, though," he said with a wink. "Mrs. Demsky will get after me if she knows I've been sneaking cookies."

Rosine scanned the office as if taking in every inch. "Are you a scientist?" she asked.

Mr. Demsky raised his chin. "I used to teach geology at the university. Now I am simply a man of faith and a store clerk. My daughter, Paloma, is the real scientist in the family. She has a PhD in mineralogy."

Even though Paloma left for college in Michigan when Cal was a baby, she still came home during holidays and summers to help out at the market. Cal loved when Paloma was working because she always let her take a candy bar for free.

Mr. Demsky turned in his chair and began digging through the pile of photos. He lifted one, using his sleeve to wipe away an inch of dust.

In the photo, Paloma wore a lab coat and peered into a giant microscope. "My girl," he said. His entire face seemed to beam with pride. "Her dissertation focused on the study of micrometeorites. Otherwise known as stardust." As curious as Cal was about how someone studied stardust, she didn't feel like it was the right time to ask. She cleared her throat. "Mr. Demsky," she began. "I'm really sorry I . . ." Her voice faded, unable to find the right words.

He replaced the photo. "Sardines are an interesting

choice." His eyes sparkled as if he were laughing at a joke that no one else heard. He handed the yellow tin to Cal. "You keep that," he said.

"It wasn't for me. It was for—"

"Wildcat," Mr. Demsky said, popping a cookie in his mouth. "Why don't you get the rest of the cans out of your sling there. Go ahead, put them in your backpack. You'll need those." Crumbs stuck in his bushy white mustache.

"How did you know?" Cal's forehead wrinkled, but she was relieved too. Wildcat depended on her.

"I know everything that happens on the mountain," he said. "Like the magic."

Cal fixed her gaze on the old man. It was as though he could read her mind. Ever since she'd overheard him talking about the meteorite the night before, she'd been aching to ask him more about the legend. Especially after what Mr. Lopez had said in class.

"Magic?" Rosine glanced at Cal. "Like what you said in class?"

"Sometimes my mouth keeps talking even when my brain wants it to stop." Cal's cheeks turned pink all over again. "I don't know why I said that."

"Because it's true, of course. You feel it, right, Cal? It's what calls you back to the mountain."

Cal swallowed hard.

Rosine shifted in her seat. "But the science teacher—Mr. Lopez—how did he say it? Wait a minute." She pulled out her notebook and began thumbing through it. "He said that the stories about the magic meteorite were fiction. Not fact."

"Lopez!" Mr. Demsky frowned as he put his left arm across his waist and pinched his chin the way Mr. Lopez did when he was in deep thought. *"Science derives from fact not fiction,"* he mimicked.

Cal almost laughed out loud at the imitation.

"What Lopez forgets is that as important as facts are to science, it is believing in the impossible—in having *faith*—that can take us to places science can't reach!"

Cal nodded as if she understood.

Mr. Demsky raised a finger. "Truth be told, meteorites have a long history of being considered mystical. There are many cultures from Native Americans to the Inuit of Greenland—all the way to ancient cultures in Greece and Rome—that believe meteorites possess spiritual qualities." He raised his bushy white eyebrows. "After all, they come to us directly from the heavens and hold secrets we are far from understanding."

"What do you mean, *mystical*?" Cal asked, hoping it meant the same as *magical*.

"I'll show you!" Mr. Demsky yanked at the bottom drawer of a rusted metal filing cabinet until it screeched open. Cal leaned over to see a wad of file folders jammed tight.

Mr. Demsky's fingers walked through what was left of their bent and torn tabs. "Here we are," he said, tugging one out. As he opened it, a cloud of dust seemed to erupt. He lifted out a stack of yellowed photographs.

"Ensisheim!" he exclaimed.

Cal wanted to respond *Gesundheit!* until she realized Mr. Demsky wasn't sneezing from the dust. He was pointing to a photo of a large ball-shaped gray rock encased in a glass box.

"This is one of the first meteorites ever discovered," he said. "It landed in 1492 in a town called Ensisheim in France." He nodded. "The good people there believed it was a message sent from God himself! In fact, King Maximilian I of Austria, who was passing through on his way to war with France, considered it a sign that his army would win in battle. It's now preserved in Regency Museum."

He handed the photo to Rosine, then held up another one. It showed a giant ball of light streaking across a town that looked as small and sleepy as Bleakerville.

"This fireball came from a small asteroid—oh, about the size of a six-story building—that broke up over the city of Chelyabinsk, Russia, on February 15, 2013. The blast was so bright it appeared as if there were a second sun in the sky. You can look it up on YouTube and actually see it happen."

Mr. Demsky put that photo down and picked up another. This one showed a shiny black stone encased in a silver bowl.

"The Black Stone of Mecca," Rosine exclaimed.

"Very good!" Mr. Demsky said.

"How did you know that?" Cal asked.

"Because I am Muslim."

"The Black Stone is built into the eastern wall of the Kaaba, a shrine within the Great Mosque of Mecca in Saudi Arabia," Mr. Demsky began. "Although it has never been tested, many believe it is a meteorite. To say that it is an object of great spiritual significance in the Muslim world would be an understatement. The mystical stone is believed to date back to the time of Adam and Eve and is the centerpiece of an ancient Muslim pilgrimage known as the Hajj—a sacred journey where worshippers kiss the stone just as the Prophet Mohammed once did."

"These are all really interesting, Mr. Demsky," Cal said. "But what about our meteorite? The one that fell on Mount Meteorite. The magic one?" She took a deep breath, doing her best to keep her emotions in check.

Rosine crossed her arms. "Is there really such a thing as a magic meteorite?"

Cal stared at her. The way Rosine asked so plainly made her realize how silly it sounded. Maybe Mom and Mr. Lopez were right. Maybe it was only a story. Maybe it was time to grow up.

Mr. Demsky folded his hands and leaned forward, his eyes sparkling like quartz. "So, you want to hear the *true* story behind the magic of Mount Meteorite?"

Yes! Cal wanted to scream. *Yes! Yes! Yes! That's what I've been saying!*

Rosine handed him the photos, and he returned them to their file folder. Then he picked up his handkerchief and coughed into it.

Cal held her breath.

"It's been fifty years now, since that day. I wasn't living in Bleakerville back then. Heck, I don't think I'd ever passed through it. Mrs. Demsky and I were newlyweds and both teaching at UConn," he said. "I remember that February morning like it was yesterday. As you know, Cal, I used to climb. Before dawn, I'd made my way to Ragged Mountain in Southington to set up top ropes. The sun was just beginning to rise. I was halfway up its face when a feeling came over me. It was as if the air had suddenly filled with electricity and my body was the conductor."

A tingle ran up Cal's spine.

"I turned to look behind me, and I could clearly make out Bleaker Mountain in the distance. Right then, the most glorious streak of green light soared across the sky. I'll tell you, it's a good thing I was anchored in, or I may have fallen." Mr. Demsky stared into space as if he could see it happening right in front of him. "The light headed straight toward the mountain and its spire, and I know for a fact that's where it landed." He blinked, turning back to the photos in his lap. "I wasn't the only one who saw it, of course. Even though it was quite early, there were other witnesses."

"You mean like the scientists who went to look for the meteorite?" Cal said. "The ones who disappeared? We talked about that in class today, but Mr. Lopez never said what happened to them."

"They died," Rosine said.

She said it like a statement, not a question, and even though she was repeating what Lexi and Tonia had said in class, this bugged Cal. "You weren't there," she said. "You don't know." She turned toward Mr. Demsky. "Is it true? Did they die?"

Mr. Demsky's bushy white eyebrows arched. "Lopez said that?"

"No," Cal said. "He told us that no one ever heard

66

from them again." She shook her head. "But people don't just disappear. I mean, even if they did die." Her forehead wrinkled. "Someone must have found something."

"Climbing equipment," Mr. Demsky said. "Gear was found in a remote cave."

Cal sat back hard in her chair. That had to be the equipment she'd found. She sucked in her breath. She wanted to believe, but the legend was like the crux of an especially difficult climb, and she felt as if she were barely holding on by her fingertips.

"How do you know that this meteorite has magic?" Rosine asked.

Not answering, Mr. Demsky slowly stood and shuffled toward the window. Without his cane, he looked as crooked as a capital *S*. He tugged on the shade, and it rolled up with such a loud *thwack*, it reminded Cal of Mr. Lopez and his yardstick.

"Because of this," Mr. Demsky said.

As if on cue, the sun hit the spire in that way that made it look like a struck matchstick. Brilliant and glowing.

Cal sighed. "Fire on ice," she murmured. "That's what it looks like to me."

"The truth is," Mr. Demsky continued, "Lopez is right. There is no proof that a meteorite fell or that it possessed magical properties." He turned toward the girls.

"But I was there. I know what I saw, and more importantly, I know what I felt." He nodded. "Like I always say, if you want to see a rock, that's what you'll see. But if you believe in magic, then that's what you'll find."

Mr. Demsky's riddles were starting to make Cal's head hurt.

"Some of us see the mountain's peak as the intersection of heaven and earth, science and faith," he continued. "There is magic on that mountain, ladies. I know it for a fact."

Cal stood. Suddenly the room felt hot and stuffy. She wanted to run away beneath the forest canopy, where she could breathe again, but something held her back. The old man knew more than he was saying. He had a secret about the mountain—about the magic—and Cal couldn't pull herself away until he shared it.

Rosine's eyes seemed to dart between the two of them as if they were speaking in a secret code that she couldn't understand. But there was no code, or if there was, only Mr. Demsky knew it. Only he held the key to this mystery.

Then Cal remembered that she knew something that Mr. Demsky didn't.

"There was a box," she said. "A wooden box. It was carved and . . . I don't know, it was special, I could tell. It had a word in it." Cal dug inside her backpack and pulled out her notebook. "Amani," she said, stretching each syllable as if to hold on to them longer.

Rosine made a small noise.

"What?" Cal asked.

Rosine stared at her feet.

Cal rolled her eyes and turned back to Mr. Demsky. "I tried to look it up, but it's not in the dictionary. I'm still trying to figure out what it means. I . . ." Cal paused, realizing what she wanted to say sounded silly, but she couldn't help herself. "I think the mountain is giving me a clue. I think it *wants* me to find the magic."

The old man scratched his chin. "Maybe. I don't know that word." He looked at Rosine, who was hugging herself. "How about you, Rosine?"

She shook her head.

Mr. Demsky winked. "Well, I'd say that you two should find out what it means."

"By climbing the spire." Cal nodded. She knew that was what had to happen. But she was also terrified to try. She looked at Mr. Demsky. "Everyone in town says it's impossible to scale."

"People said it was impossible to free-climb the technical route on El Capitan called the Nose until Lynn Hill did it. And they said a woman couldn't summit Everest until Junko Tabei proved them wrong," Mr. Demsky scoffed. "Lots of things are *impossible*—until someone goes ahead and does them anyway."

Cal bit her lip.

"I've seen you climb, Cal. What makes you think you couldn't scale the spire?"

She stared at her feet.

"The astrophysicist Neil deGrasse Tyson once pointed out that each of us has as many atoms in a single molecule of DNA as there are stars in the galaxy. Each of you girls is your own little universe. I'd say you could do anything."

Cal took a deep breath. Mr. Demsky's talk was making her feel tired and confused. She was done with his riddles. She needed facts, direction. It was as if the old man knew what she wanted, knew what she *needed*—but was dangling the truth just out of her reach.

"How do *I* find the magic?" she demanded. "What do *I* do?"

"When you believe . . . that's when the impossible becomes possible. That's when you'll find the magic."

"What am I supposed to believe in?" Cal asked.

But Mr. Demsky left her question hanging in the air. "I best go check on Abner. Make sure he hasn't chased away any more customers today."

Chapter 8

After Mr. Demsky left the room, Cal and Rosine gathered their backpacks and made their way through the store. When they were outside, Cal stared up at the spire. Then took off running.

Soon Rosine had caught up and was jogging next to her.

"You don't have to stay with me," Cal said loudly. She was starting to feel winded.

"I know," Rosine yelled back. "I want to."

Cal sped up.

Rosine did too.

As they came to the Demskys' cottage, Cal felt a stitch in her side.

"Wasn't that your house back there?" Rosine asked.

Cal clutched her stomach.

"You're going too fast," Rosine said. "Walking will stop the pain."

"I know what I'm doing," Cal said, but she slowed. "You're not from around here, are you?"

"No," Rosine said.

"Where are you from?" Cal asked.

"Central Africa," Rosine said. "I was born in the Democratic Republic of Congo, but I spent most of my life in Burundi."

"Why did you leave?"

"There was a war in my country. It wasn't safe for us."

"Why'd you come to Bleakerville?"

"First, we lived in Elm City for almost a year. But I didn't like it. There was too much noise—people, cars, sirens—day and night. I wanted to be somewhere . . . peaceful. Then Mali lost her job, and we had to leave our apartment. Mr. and Mrs. Demsky and their synagogue offered to host us in Bleakerville, so we came to live here in their carriage house." Rosine grinned. "I love it here."

"Who's Mali?"

"My sister. She's nineteen, but she acts like an old woman. She's always telling me what to do and that I should obey her." They'd reached the stone walkway that led to the carriage house's front door. Rosine stopped. "I'll see you tomorrow?"

Cal gave a quick nod. "Okay."

Before the words were even out of her mouth, she began running again. She continued up Mountain Road until she reached the place where the pavement narrowed and turned to dirt. She slapped the yellow sign, leaving its gong-like vibration behind her as she ducked beneath the forest canopy.

It was getting dark quickly, and she scolded herself for not leaving Demsky's Market sooner. But Cal knew the way by heart. When she got to the ledge, she hugged the mountain with her working arm. Then scooted across its pencil-thin ridge until she reached Wildcat's boulder. She jumped onto the rock platform, then headed inside the cave.

As her eyes slowly adjusted to the cave's darkness, she let her backpack slide from her shoulder. She opened it and dug out the sardine tins. She still felt guilty for taking them, but what was she supposed to do? *Wildcat needs food. I had no choice.* She stacked the cans against the wall, saving one to peel open.

"Wildcat!" she called.

Almost immediately there was a sound of rustling leaves outside.

"Wildcat?"

But even in the darkness of the cave, Cal could see that the shadow that appeared at the cave's entrance was not cat-shaped. It was person-shaped.

"Wh-who are you?" she shouted.

The shadow didn't budge.

"Wh-what do you want?"

There was no sound except for the chattering of teeth. Then, "It's me."

"Rosine?" Cal said.

The new girl stepped inside.

"You followed me? This is my cave. It's private."

Rosine placed a hand on her hip. "We're in a cave. On a mountain. Explain to me what's so private about that."

Cal's eyebrows furrowed. "No one knows about this cave. No one can even get here but me."

"I'm here," Rosine said.

"How did you get across the ridge in those sandals?"

Before Rosine could answer, there was another loud rustling noise.

"Ahhhhh!" Rosine screamed. "Get off!"

Wildcat had leapt onto her shoulder.

"Wildcat!" Cal shouted. "No!"

The cat jumped down, making his gurgly-purr sound

as if to say, *Calm down! I was only saying hello. Now, where's my supper?*

Cal sucked in her breath. She wasn't sure if she was angrier at Rosine for overreacting or at Wildcat for choosing Rosine's shoulder instead of hers.

"Come here, you." Cal plucked out a sardine.

Rosine crept closer. "You are friends with this stray cat?"

"It's Wildcat. He won't hurt you." Cal fed him the fish.

"Can I feed him?"

"Umm. Okay, I guess. Hold out your hand." Cal dug out another fish and placed it in Rosine's hand.

Wildcat gobbled it up, then licked Rosine's palm. She giggled.

When Wildcat finished, he brushed a furry cheek against Rosine's knee.

"He likes it if you scratch behind his ear," Cal said.

Wildcat purred as Rosine pet him.

Now Cal's teeth began to chatter.

Rosine removed her backpack and dug inside it. "The reason I followed you is because after you left, I remembered I never gave you this." She pulled out Lexi's pink sweatshirt.

Cal blinked. "Is this some kind of joke?"

"No."

Cal stared at her suspiciously. "I don't want it."

Rosine's gaze fell to the ground.

Cal was starting to get angry all over again. *Why couldn't this girl mind her own business? And now she'd found Wildcat's secret cave!* The familiar ember of anger ignited.

"Why did you do that?" Cal asked.

"Because you were cold."

Cal blinked at this answer. There was something raw about this girl. She wasn't wrong. Cal was cold. She'd been cold in school when she took off the sweatshirt, and she was cold right then, sitting inside a dark cave as the sun set.

"You could have given it to me tomorrow." Cal stared hard at Rosine. "Tell me the truth. Why are you really here?"

Wildcat sauntered outside. The girls watched him leave.

"You wouldn't understand."

"Try me."

"What does that mean, *try me*?" Rosine asked.

"It means, tell me what the problem is, and maybe . . . I don't know . . . I'll understand."

Rosine glanced around the cave as if it held the

answer she was searching for. She sighed. "My sister, Mali," she finally said. "I want to find the magic for her."

"Is she sick?"

"She's sick with sadness, and she's making bad decisions for us. She wants us to move again to another city. She says this quiet town makes her more sad and lonely, but we came here only this week." Rosine bit her lip. "I need the magic to make her want to stop moving and stay here in Bleakerville."

Cal rolled her eyes. "Why would you want to stay here?"

"All my life I have never felt I am home. We have always been moving. Now," Rosine said, "I want to stand still."

"Why aren't your parents helping?" Cal asked.

"My parents . . . they are gone."

"Oh." Cal immediately felt terrible for asking. "I'm sorry."

Rosine stood up. "You did nothing wrong. What are you sorry for?"

"I don't know. It's just something you say, right?"

"I don't say that."

Cal wasn't used to the way this girl thought and talked, but she liked it. Rosine said exactly what she meant. Plain and honest.

"I think we should climb the spire together," Rosine said.

"I'm not sure." Cal picked up the empty sardine tin and put it in a plastic bag in her backpack to throw out later.

She headed outside and Rosine followed. Wildcat was sitting on his boulder, licking a paw.

The spire's profile looked even taller against the orange sky.

"You're not sure about what?" Rosine asked.

Cal raised her chin. "I work alone."

"You don't trust me."

"That's not it," Cal said.

"You are scared," Rosine said.

Cal turned on her. "No, I'm not."

"Of course you are. I've climbed lots of mountains, and *I'm* scared." She pointed toward the stone tower. Its peak had disappeared inside a cloud. "It goes up forever."

"So, what if I am?"

"If we do it together, we will both be less scared."

Cal rolled her eyes. "You say that, but you don't know what you're talking about. I mean, look at your shoes. You can't climb in sandals."

"When we were in Burundi, I lived near a mountain. I spent a lot of time there. I know what I'm doing."

"I'll think about it," Cal said. "Right now you can show

me what a good climber you are by making your way back across the ridge. It's getting dark."

"No problem," Rosine said as she scrambled onto the boulder where Wildcat was now lounging. "Bye, Wildcat."

"See you tomorrow," Cal said, scratching behind his floppy ear.

Wildcat purred as if saying, *Don't be late!*

Rosine laughed. "He's a funny cat," she said.

"Yes, he is." Cal looked at Rosine. "So. Let's see what you got."

Rosine shimmied across the ridge in a few light steps.

Cal followed, jumping down behind her.

"Okay, you managed that, but it doesn't mean you can scale the spire," Cal said. "It's as tall as a ten-story building."

Rosine shrugged. "I'm not going to let that stop me," she said as she headed into the forest.

Cal's forehead wrinkled. She still didn't understand this girl, but somehow, she felt a connection too. Even though they were from opposite sides of the world, even though they wanted different things, there was something familiar about Rosine.

"Hey!" Cal shouted. "Wait! Maybe I could use that sweatshirt after all!"

Rosine turned and tossed it to her.

Cal pulled it on over her too-small T-shirt. "And now that I think about it, I have a pair of boots in the cave that might fit you."

Even though Cal couldn't see Rosine's face, somehow she knew Rosine was smiling.

After leaving Rosine at the carriage house, Cal darted across the Demskys' lawn, ducking low in case the couple was outside again. Fortunately, the front porch was empty.

She hopped up her own front steps, checking to see what Mrs. Demsky may have left for dinner, but there was nothing there.

As she was about to open the front door, she heard voices. She paused, pressing an ear against the door.

"Does Cal know yet?"

It was Mrs. Demsky's voice.

"No, we're going to see him tomorrow, and I'll tell her after that."

"I don't understand why the doctors won't do the surgery."

Her mother's voice seemed to falter. "They think it's too late."

"But they have to try."

Inside her mother's silence, Cal held her breath. *Was Mom crying?*

"Not if it won't help," Mom finally said.

"What can we do, Elaine?" Mrs. Demsky asked.

"Be there for Cal. That's all I care about. She holds everything in . . . I worry about her, and I don't know how much longer I can do this."

"How about Simon's parents? Are they able to help out? Or Viola? Can she stay with you again?"

"Simon's father isn't well. Both of his parents are frail. And Viola's been wonderful, but she has her own family to take care of. I can't ask her to move in again." There was a pause. "I need to know Cal will be okay if I don't . . ." She broke down into tears.

Don't what? Cal wondered.

Then she understood.

If I don't make it.

That was what Mom was saying.

Her mother didn't think she was ever going to get better.

Cal felt as if someone had gut-punched her. She spun away. Running.

She didn't know where she was headed, and she didn't care.

Chapter 9

The next morning, Cal met Rosine at the bus stop.

Even though Cal didn't say a word, Rosine seemed to understand what she needed. The two stood silently waiting for the bus. When it came, they shared a seat.

At school, Cal made her way to homeroom feeling as if she were in a trance. The hallways held their usual chaos, but Cal couldn't hear anything. She couldn't see anything. Part of her felt frozen in time, still crouched outside her front door hearing what she wished she'd never heard.

Last night, after she'd run off, she ended up sitting alone on the steps of Demsky's closed market, staring at the mountain until she was sure her mother had fallen asleep.

She couldn't face her.

Of course, she'd known Mom was sick. Really sick. But she'd been sick plenty of times with colds, the flu, even pneumonia once. She always got better. Always.

The idea that her mother wouldn't get better . . . couldn't get better . . . was impossible.

Impossible to imagine.

And impossible to face.

But there it was. Sitting right in front of her, as big and tall and terrifying as the spire itself.

"Please," she'd begged the spire as she sat on the market's steps. "Please help me find your magic so I can help my mom."

But for all her planning and plotting and mapping, deep down, Cal knew she couldn't face the spire any more than she could face her mother's illness.

You're such a coward, *Cal Scott,* she scolded herself. *And you'll always be one.*

"Cal! Cal!" Ms. Adelman, the gym teacher, snapped her out of her loop of sadness.

"Come here—you've got to see this!" Ms. Adelman waved her over before walking into the gym.

Cal followed.

"Climbing walls?" Cal asked. "Where did they come from?"

"Isn't it great? The guys from Stone Age Rock Gym got new equipment. They're donating what they don't need to the school to encourage kids to learn to climb. They've even provided harnesses and climbing shoes. It's incredible!"

Cal hugged her casted arm. She felt too numb to get excited about anything.

"You have gym today, right?" Ms. Adelman asked.

Cal nodded.

"Excellent!" Ms. Adelman said. "I'm so lucky I have an experienced climber like you in my class. I know you're grounded right now because of your arm, but can you help me teach kids how to tie knots and use the gear properly?"

Cal nodded again.

"Perfect! See you then!" Ms. Adelman said.

Later that morning, Cal's class stood against the mats that lined the gymnasium's walls. Cal stared in admiration. The climbing wall really was beautiful. Colorful plastic fixtures of different sizes dotted its length from floor to ceiling—bright reds, cerulean blues, sunshine yellows.

Ms. Adelman blew her whistle. Dressed in baggy gray sweats, many students underestimated her strength, but not Cal. She'd seen her climb.

"Today, we'll start by learning to tie secure knots. It's one of the most important parts of climbing," Ms. Adelman told the class. "Everyone pair up and grab a rope to share. Also, grab a harness and climbing shoes."

Pair up. Two words that made Cal feel as though she'd swallowed a rock. She grabbed her gear, then stared at the floor, waiting to see who else ended up as the odd man out.

When she looked up, Rosine stood in front of her.

"Do you know how to put this on?" Rosine held up a harness.

"You step into it like it's a pair of pants," Cal said.

Rosine began to lift a leg, but she was holding the harness backward.

"No, like this." Cal helped her step in, then tightened and double-backed the buckles with her good hand.

Ms. Adelman was suddenly in front of them. "Cal," she said. "Can I borrow you and . . ." She stared at Rosine.

"Rosine Kanambe," Rosine said, lifting her chin.

"What a lovely name. Follow me, girls!"

Kids whispered as Cal and Rosine stood beneath a set of ropes that dangled from a hook at the top of the wall.

Ms. Adelman handed each girl one end of the rope. Turning back to the other students, she blew her whistle.

Rosine jumped.

"Pay attention, everyone!" Ms. Adelman said. "We are going to learn how to top rope. First you need to secure your rope to your harness. Everyone, dangle the rope in front of you and make a small bend, or bight, in the rope about four feet from the end." Ms. Adelman held up the empty loop. "Here's my guy," she said. "I'm going to take the tail end of the rope and give him a tie." She wrapped the tail end over the bight.

Kids laughed.

"Now I'm going to poke him in the eye." Ms. Adelman threaded the rope through the loop. "You should have a figure eight in your hand. Cal, can you walk around and check?"

Cal showed kids how to fix their knots, and she adjusted others.

"Okay," Ms. Adelman said. "You have two tie-in points on your harness—one at the legs and one at the waist. First you want to thread the tail end of your rope through the lower loop, then the upper loop. Next, trace it along the same path as the first figure eight. The knot should be a fist's length from your harness."

Cal checked Rosine's. "Two, four, six, eight, ten," she

said, making sure the rope was tied right. Then she flipped it over and counted again. "You got it."

"I don't need the rope," Rosine said. "I can climb without it."

"You do too need it," Cal scoffed. "Being even four feet off the ground doubles your weight if you fall to the ground."

"I won't fall," Rosine said.

Cal was trying to figure out if Rosine really knew what she was doing or if she was showing off. "There's no way you'll climb that without falling."

"How do you know? You've never seen me climb. Maybe you're worried you can't do it."

Cal studied Rosine. *Was that a dare?*

"Okay, we're ready!" Ms. Adelman was back. "Who wants to go first?"

Cal and Rosine raised their hands.

"You have a broken arm, Cal. I'm sure you could handle this wall with one hand tied behind your back, but you know I can't let you."

Cal frowned.

"Rosine, you want to give it a try?"

"Yes," Rosine said, chin high.

Ms. Adelman blew her whistle again. "Everyone pay attention!" she shouted. "I'm going to belay Rosine." She untied Cal's knots and threaded them through the belay device attached to her harness.

"First thing we do is double-check to make sure our ropes are straight and knots are secure. Follow the ropes with your eyes from Rosine's harness," she said, checking the figure eight, "up the wall to the anchor on the ceiling, then back down, threaded correctly through my belay device to the stopper knot at the end. Perfect."

Ms. Adelman took a belayer's stance, feet separated and knees slightly bent.

"When that's done and Rosine is ready, she'll say, *On belay?*"

Rosine faced the wall, scanning it from bottom to top. "On belay?"

"Belay on," Ms. Adelman responded.

"Now you say, *Climbing!* And when I respond, you start," Ms. Adelman said.

"Climbing!" Rosine said.

"Climb on," Ms. Adelman replied.

Rosine grabbed ahold of two colored features and pulled herself onto the wall. She moved slowly at first, making careful choices as she placed her hands and feet. The higher she went, the more confident she seemed to grow.

Cal became mesmerized by Rosine's movements. It was as if she were dancing upward in some kind of climbing ballet. Quick and light as a feather, she stretched her legs and arms in impossible directions until she was at the top.

Kids clapped.

"Wonderful!" Ms. Adelman called.

Rosine looked down, grinning.

"Are you ready to be lowered?" Ms. Adelman asked.

"Ready."

"Face the wall with your feet against it and your legs straight. Now kind of lower your butt, as if you were sitting. When you're ready, you can say, *Ready to lower!* Then I'll start feeding you the rope I took in when you were climbing. As you feel your body lower, start walking backward down the wall. We'll keep that going, nice and easy, okay? Remember, I got you."

When Rosine got into position, she shouted, "Ready to lower!"

"Lowering!" Ms. Adelman pulled back the lever on the belay device so that the rope she had taken in as Rosine climbed now threaded back out—slow and even. At first Rosine's shoulders seemed to hunch in surprise when her body began to lower, but she quickly caught on, walking backward down the wall as if she'd done it a million times. When she was a couple feet from the ground, she jumped onto the floor mat.

"Well done!" Ms. Adelman gave Rosine a high five. The class applauded again. "Who's next?"

As Luis took a turn climbing, Cal walked over to Rosine.

"Where did you learn to climb like that?"

"I told you. I spent a lot of time on mountains. Plus, you're not a kid in Burundi unless you've climbed many papaya trees." Rosine laughed.

"For me it's apple trees."

"That sounds fun too," Rosine said.

Cal nodded. "Well, you're really good."

"Does that mean you're ready to trust me on the spire?"

Cal stared at her feet and then at Rosine. She had run out of excuses and was starting to feel as if she'd been caught in a lie. "I told you," she said. "I work alone." She walked away.

As the bell rang and kids began leaving, Cal stayed behind, tying and untying her rope. Something about that simple movement brought her back to the mountain . . . and her dad. A memory began to fill her head.

She was eight years old, standing at the base of Ragged Mountain with her father and his climbing friends.

Mountains are living, breathing things, Cal, he'd said, staring up at the one-hundred-foot face. *When I'm on the mountain, I feel more alive than anywhere else.*

Before the sun had risen, they'd parked, then hiked the Metacomet Trail in. It was a cool September morning, and the scents of damp earth, lichen, and the mountain's traprock filled her head.

Cal loved the feeling of being with her dad's climbing group. They acted like one big family. Everyone called each other by their last names—Lopez, Crutcher, Adelman, McGuire, Demsky. Even then Mr. Demsky was old, but he still came to support the others. Cal loved the way they included her, calling her by her last name too—Scott. Same as her dad.

She'd always felt more comfortable with adults than kids her own age, and no one in the group ever talked down to her or tried to make things easier. They treated her like an equal.

At the same time, she was nervous. As she gazed at the mountain, it suddenly appeared higher and more challenging than she remembered.

"You ready?" Dad asked as he checked Cal's knots. "Two, four, six, eight, ten," he counted, making sure they were tied securely.

Cal nodded.

"Okay. You know what to do. Take your time and study each spot before you make your move. Remember, you might look at the rock one moment, and it will seem like there's nowhere to go and that all that's left is to quit and fall. But if you're patient and examine it carefully, you'll find its weaknesses—a crack, a crevice, a knob. Next thing you know, you'll have found your way up." He paused. "And, Cal . . ."

"Uh-huh," she said, still staring up at the jagged rock.

"Remember, I'm always here on the other end, and I'm never letting go."

Cal's legs that never seemed to stop moving suddenly wouldn't budge.

"Go on," he urged. "Start by facing the mountain."

She inspected the rock in front of her—gray and ragged like the mountain's name.

"You got this, Cal."

She reached out and, fitting her hands in cracks, stepped onto the skinniest of edges. She was on the mountain.

"Awesome," Dad cheered. "First step's the hardest. Keep going!"

Hand. Foot. Hand. Foot. Cal felt her body moving upward.

"Woot! Woot!" her dad called.

Reach. Stretch. Hand. Foot. Reach. Stretch. Foot.

The world seemed to fall away until all that was left was her and the mountain.

Foot. Hand. Stretch. Hand. Foot.

Then she stopped.

There didn't seem to be any more holds she could reach. Every muscle in her forearms strained. She was going to lose her grip soon if she didn't find a new hold. She looked down. Her father appeared so small, so far away.

"Look up!" her father called. "Don't look down, look up!"

She began to panic. Her eyes blurred.

"I can't do it! Falling!" she called down.

"Fall away," her father replied.

Cal let go, immediately feeling the pull of her father on the other end of the rope. She dangled in place.

The mountain seemed to mock her. *You don't have what it takes.*

"I want to come down!" she shouted.

"Relax, Cal. I got you. Take a minute. Rest. Study the mountain."

Cal breathed. Dangling there, fifty feet from the ground, she squinted, still not finding a path upward.

She was about to yell, *Ready to lower!* so her dad

would lower her, when a cloud shifted and a ray of sunshine illuminated a new spot. There was a pocket to her right that she hadn't noticed a second ago. She reached, barely gripping it by her fingertips.

She was back on the mountain.

"That's it!" her father said, pulling the slack. "You got it. Keep going!"

Suddenly more flaws appeared—cracks, crevices, knobs. Up. Up. Up. She climbed until she came to a thick ledge near the top.

"Woooooot!" her father shouted, followed by hoots and hollers from the rest of the climbers, who were already on their way back down.

"Woot! Woot! Woot! Ah-ah-wooooo!"

She rested on the ridge, feeling her body explode with emotion. *I did it!* she thought. *I really did it!*

She could feel her father's secure grip on the rope, and that gave her enough confidence to take in the view.

The world looked completely different from the top of Ragged Mountain. The horizon was layered with browns and greens and blues. When she squinted, she could even make out the peak of Mount Meteorite's spire in the distance.

"Ready to come down?" her father called.

Cal faced the mountain. She got in sitting position,

legs straight, feet against the mountain. "Ready to lower!" she shouted.

"Lowering!" he responded.

Cal walked down backward until her feet touched the ground.

"You did it, Cal!" Her father gave her a giant bear hug.

She buried her face in his jacket and breathed. He smelled like the mountain. "Thanks, Dad. I couldn't have done it without you."

"I told you, sweetheart. I'm never letting go."

Brriiiinnnggg.

The sound of the bell announcing the start of lunch jolted Cal from her daydream. She could hear Ms. Adelman talking to students in the hallway. She dropped the rope into the bin and snuck out the back.

As she passed a window, she paused. There was Mount Meteorite. Watching her.

As her gaze followed the spire to its peak, Rosine's voice filled her head.

Does that mean you're ready to trust me on the spire?

But the real question was whether Cal trusted herself.

Could I really do it? she wondered.

She knew one person who'd tell her the truth.

Chapter 10

Cal made her way to the science room, opening the door wide enough to peek inside.

Mr. Lopez sat at his desk with his feet up, a book in one hand and an apple in the other.

Cal knocked.

"Scott!" Mr. Lopez exclaimed. He put the book down. "Am I allowed to call you that when no one is around?"

Cal nodded sheepishly.

"You know, you shouldn't let those girls bother you. They got nothing on you, kiddo." When she didn't respond, he pulled a chair over. "Join me. Did you bring lunch?"

Cal shook her head. "I came to ask a question."

"Ask away," he said, taking a bite of his apple.

"It's about Mount Meteorite . . . and the spire."

"Okayyyy."

"How come no climbers ever attempt to scale the spire . . . I mean, besides the guys who disappeared?"

He shrugged. "Word's spread it's impossible, I guess."

"But that's never stopped the climbers who live for the adventure. The true dirtbaggers. They love the challenge. Why don't they climb it?"

Mr. Lopez laughed. "Well . . . first of all . . . no one can find Bleakerville."

Cal frowned at his attempt to be funny.

He cleared his throat. "The truth is, it's a small mountain in a remote place, and frankly . . . the spire isn't that special for most people. Those rock stars are looking to climb the giants—El Cap and Joshua Tree and the Tetons."

"But what about climbers around here?"

"Mount Meteorite doesn't compare to other New England areas. Cathedral Ledge, the Gunks, Smugglers' Notch . . . the list goes on and on." Mr. Lopez shrugged.

"But none of those things make it impossible."

"The first pitch doesn't look bad. But then the spire

does turn smooth as glass." He tossed his apple core in the trash. "What is it you really want to know, Scott?"

"I want to know about the meteorite. The magic. I—I know you don't believe the legend, but Mr. Demsky says he saw the meteor—he talks about the way the light touched the mountain in a way that was . . ."

"Magical?"

"Yeah," Cal said. "And I feel it, Mr. Lopez. Every single time I'm on the mountain." She looked at her teacher with expectant eyes.

He nodded. "You know, Demsky was my teacher too . . . like, a hundred years ago. He's practically family, so I can say with confidence that he's full of beans on this."

"How do you explain the light?"

"Lots of things could have caused that—lightning or headlights coming from the interstate."

"It wasn't headlights, and it wasn't lightning," Cal scoffed. "Mr. Demsky said the light stretched across the sky, heading straight for the spire."

"Okay, I can see you're demanding evidence here." He reached for his computer's mouse. "A trait I do enjoy seeing in my scientists . . ." He typed into the search bar. "Here's my theory. Ohsumi."

"Oh-what?" Cal asked.

He rotated the screen toward her. It showed an object that looked like a large black ball with a shiny silver cap and two long antennae.

"In the 1960s," Mr. Lopez said, "countries began sending satellites into space. On February eleventh, 1970, Japan launched their first. It was called Ohsumi."

Cal stared at the image. "It looks kind of like a robot."

Mr. Lopez nodded. "Satellites mimic meteors, especially during sunrise or sunset when they're more likely to catch the sun and reflect its rays." He sniffed. "In my opinion, what Demsky saw on February twelfth—the day after Ohsumi launched—was exactly that. The satellite reflecting the sun. An illusion."

"But Mr. Demsky said the light was green."

Mr. Lopez shrugged. "People see what they want to see. The problem is that Demsky has no evidence to back up his claim." He clicked off the image, leaving a blank screen. "Sorry to be the one to tell you, Scott, but there's no magic on the spire. I know it for a fact."

The bell rang.

"I have to go," she said.

"Stop by anytime." Mr. Lopez began collecting papers on his desk. "And let me know if you or your mom ever need anything."

Cal started for the door, then paused. "Mr. Lopez, do you think I could . . . you know, scale the spire?"

"You're a good climber, Scott, but the spire?" His eyebrows arched. "It's extremely difficult." He shook his head. "You should ask your dad that question. Okay?"

Cal headed into the hallway.

As she walked past the gym, she peeked through the open door, once again admiring the new colorful climbing wall. She hugged her casted arm, then stepped inside.

There was something about her conversation with Mr. Lopez that ignited the tiniest spark somewhere deep inside.

She made her way over to the bins filled with climbing shoes and harnesses.

If we do it together, we will both be less scared.

She thought about how Rosine danced her way up the wall, graceful as a ballerina.

That girl is not afraid of anything, Cal thought. She wondered what that would be like. Facing impossible things as if they were no big deal.

You're a good climber, Scott, but the spire?

Cal frowned. *Mr. Lopez doesn't know anything.* She leaned over a bin. The shoes she'd worn earlier sat on top. She looked over her shoulder. The gym was empty.

She opened her backpack and tucked the shoes inside, along with a harness.

She began to head toward the door, when she had another thought. She darted back and grabbed a second pair of shoes and another harness.

Then she ran.

Chapter 11

Later that afternoon, after the bus had dropped them off, Cal and Rosine headed up Mountain Road together.

"Do you want to help me feed Wildcat?" Cal asked. "You can try on the extra boots I keep in the cave. If they fit, you can have them."

"Thank you! Yes, I want to go. We can make more plans for the spire."

Cal took a deep breath. "Can I tell you a secret?" She'd never admitted to anyone how she'd been taking stuff lately. Things she had no right taking. But there was something about Rosine that made Cal think she might understand. Or not judge her, anyway.

"Of course," Rosine replied. But before Cal could confess, a horn beeped.

Cal looked up to see her mother's gray pickup parked on the side of the road, the engine running. The driver's side window opened.

"Where are you going, Cal?" a woman called. "I've been waiting for you."

Cal did a double take before recognizing her own mother. Long, wavy red hair replaced the cap she wore at home. Cal had only seen Mom wear the wig when she'd first bought it. *If I can't look like myself,* she said with a wink, *I'm going to look like Julia Roberts in* Pretty Woman. Then she drew on eyebrows that Cal thought gave her kind of a surprised look and tinged her cheeks and lips pink.

"Hello," Mrs. Scott said when she noticed Rosine. "You're staying at the Demskys' carriage house, right?"

"Yes, ma'am," Rosine said.

"I'm sorry I haven't been up yet to meet you and your sister."

Rosine smiled broadly. "Please come anytime. Mali will love to meet you."

Mrs. Scott nodded. "Unfortunately, we can't today. We're late for . . . an appointment. Okay, Cal. We need to go."

"What appointment?" Cal asked.

"I told you. Visiting hours. Dad," Mrs. Scott said, clearly embarrassed to mention prison in front of Rosine.

"And *I* told you *I* wasn't going." Cal turned and continued walking up the road. Rosine didn't seem to know what to do.

"Calliope Rose Scott, get in the truck right now," Mrs. Scott said loudly, clearly not worried about politeness anymore.

Cal spun around and stomped her foot. She hated how it made her feel as if she were five years old, but she couldn't help it. She wanted to kick the door.

Her mother gripped the steering wheel with both hands and leaned forward until her forehead rested on it. "Please, Cal," she said. "Please just get in the truck."

Cal looked longingly at the mountain, then rolled her eyes. "Fine. One sec." She walked back to Rosine. "Can you feed Wildcat?" she whispered. "There's a stack of sardine tins in the cave."

Rosine nodded. "Yes. I will do that."

"Thanks . . . and don't forget to try on the boots." Cal walked around the front of the truck and climbed into the passenger seat.

Mom waved to Rosine before driving off. "What was all that about?"

Cal didn't answer.

Her mother breathed deeply. "I know you hate this, Cal, but he's still your dad." Her voice seemed to catch. She sniffed. "And we're still a family. We will get through this." The way Mom's forehead wrinkled made Cal think that she didn't believe her own words.

Her mother cleared her throat. "What time did you get home last night?" she asked. "I don't like not seeing you after school. Mrs. Demsky brought beef stew. Did you have some?" She bit her lip. "I'm sorry I keep falling asleep so early. You still need to eat a good dinner, okay?"

Cal shrugged as her mind traveled to the conversation she'd overheard the night before.

Mom sighed. "Are you going to give me the silent treatment all the way to the prison?"

"No."

As they pulled onto the highway, the gentle hum of the pickup helped Cal relax a bit. She glanced at her mother's profile. Her face looked tiny inside her fake big hair. She knew Mom didn't want to go to the prison either. But she was doing it. And she wasn't complaining.

"You look nice," Cal said, her voice a low whisper.

Mom grinned. "That's my girl."

Cal wanted to smile back, but she couldn't even muster an inside smile. The same force that pulled the corners of her mouth into a frown was at work again. It was a force she didn't have the strength to fight.

She wanted to be her mother's girl. She wanted things to be the way they used to be. She suddenly wished she could put some makeup on their life. Some blush to make their dull-green house look rosy. Some concealer to hide the moldy roof and crooked shutters. But at the same time, she knew it wouldn't matter. It wasn't hard to see that her mom was still pale beneath her makeup. She could paint over the dark circles under her eyes, but they still looked hollow and tired. And no matter how hard Mom tried to smile, the twitch at the corners of her mouth told Cal that she was fighting her own dark forces.

Soon they got off the highway and were driving past long fences topped with razor wire. Davison Correctional Institution reminded Cal of a haunted house, with its concrete columns and faded brick. A man out front was raking leaves. He wore a khaki jumper with PRISONER boldly stamped on the back. As they drove into the parking lot, he winked at Cal. She quickly turned away.

"Here," Mom said, handing Cal a mask. She put it on as they exited the truck. Cal followed her mom up the granite steps and through the large columns. Inside there was a metal detector. "Please empty your pockets into the container and fill this out," a woman in a black uniform said to Mom as she handed her a paper. "Also, you'll need to show her birth certificate," the officer said, pointing at Cal.

Her mother put her phone and keys in the plastic dish and walked through. The woman handed her a key with a large plastic tag. "You can't bring phones inside," she said. "You'll have to put that in a locker. When you're done with your form, go to the window."

Cal walked through the machine and took a seat on a chipped orange plastic chair while her mother filled out paperwork. When Mom had finished, she stood in front of a window that Cal couldn't see into. The frosted glass slid open with a snap, and a man took the paper. "We'll call you when you can go in."

After Mom locked up her phone, she sat next to Cal and took her hand. She pointed at the cast. "Almost done," she said. "Only a few more days until it comes off."

Cal didn't answer. Instead, she looked around the room. A woman sat near them wearing a party dress and tall spikey heels. The dress was short and silver and reflected the light when she moved. A few seats away, another woman sat with a fussy baby on her lap. Every now and then the young mom stood and walked around, patting the baby gently and cooing. An elderly woman wearing a heavy coat and scarf fingered a set of beads and whispered to herself.

"Scott," a man called. He was dressed in black and wore a badge that read CORRECTIONS OFFICER.

Mom stood. "Right here. We're right here."

Cal thought her voice sounded different—high-pitched and strained.

"Stand here." He pointed to a square marked out in black tape on the floor. After he'd gathered the lady in the party dress and the old woman, he spoke into his radio. The sound of grinding metal made Cal jump. A gray steel door cranked open.

"Step forward," the man ordered when the opening was wide enough. In front of them was another heavy steel door.

As soon as everyone was inside, the door that had just opened began to close behind them. "What's happening?"

"It's okay, Cal," Mom whispered.

The door slammed into the wall with a sickening *kerthunk* that seemed to vibrate throughout Cal's body. It was as if they were inside an elevator that didn't go anywhere. The woman in the party dress pulled at her hem. The old woman clutched her beads. Cal shut her eyes against the sticky smells of perfume and body odor. Her mother reached over and tried to hold her hand, but Cal yanked it away.

Even though nothing was moving, the walls felt as if they were closing in on her. Her breath became shallow and labored. That place—that room—was stifling her. She worked to picture her mountain with its trees and dirt smells.

Just when Cal thought her heart was about to leap straight out of her body, the door in front of them slowly cranked open. Cal opened her eyes as light poured in from a large room. It reminded her of the cafeteria at school. It was empty except for rows of tables. But these tables were steel, and each had a red stripe down the middle. A man dressed in the same khaki uniform as the guy she'd seen raking stood behind each table.

At first, the men appeared almost identical, but when she really looked, she saw that some wore ponytails and some had buzz cuts. Some were tall, and some were short. They were white and brown and black. She scanned each one until she found him. His hair was cut short, and he looked thin. Even though he was wearing a mask too, she could tell his mustache and beard had been shaved. His thick black glasses were taped at the corner.

He gazed up at Mom, his eyes gray and serious. Cal watched his chest rise and fall in deep breaths as if he were struggling for air too.

Mom headed toward his table. "Come on, Cal," she said.

Cal sat on a round metal stool that was bolted to the floor. Another corrections officer came over. "Don't cross the line," he said, pointing at the red tape that separated Dad's side of the table from Cal and her mother's.

"Cal," her father said.

She stared at his hands, neatly folded, and immediately noticed how clean they were. Before COVID-19, when he still worked as a mechanic at Arthur's Auto Repair, her dad's hands were always dirty with grease. Even after that, as he found odd jobs fixing tractors and farm equipment, it seemed that no matter how hard he scrubbed his fingernails, he couldn't get rid of the black. Right then, sitting in that prison, his hands looked as if they'd been soaked in bleach. It seemed as if she were looking at a stranger's hands.

He cleared his throat. "I'm sorry you had to come here."

"She wanted to," Mom lied. "Right, Cal?"

Cal couldn't look away from those clean pink fingernails.

"Is . . . Is your arm feeling better?" he asked.

Cal cradled her cast.

Mom tugged at her right earlobe. "How are you, Simon? Really? This place . . ." Her words seemed to dissolve.

"It's . . . I'm getting used to it. Thirty-seven days in, not that I'm counting." He tried to force a laugh, but it seemed to get stuck in his throat.

Mom swallowed hard. "You look good," she said. "But too thin."

"I've been working out a bit. Push-ups, you know." He tried to smile, but it didn't last. "There isn't much to do. I read as much as I can. Sometimes it's not so bad. Lots of time to think."

"Is the food horrible?"

Her father laughed. "Yeah. But that's okay."

"I talked to your lawyer. Everything has been filed, and she's really optimistic about . . . the petition. She told me she would know something later today."

"With everything else you have going on. I'm so sorry." Dad took a deep breath. "Enough about that. How are *you*, Lainey? I mean, really." His forehead wrinkled. "Was the chemo pretty bad this time?"

"It was fine. The steroids keep me jumpy . . . then tired. I'll probably crash tomorrow."

Cal looked up to see her father's face disappear in his new, clean hands. A muffled noise came from them. She sucked in her breath. She'd never seen her father cry before. Mom reached out and put her hand on his lowered head. The corrections officer was immediately there. "No contact, ma'am."

"Oh," Mom said. "I'm sorry. I forgot . . . It's a habit, you know."

"Don't do it again," he said before marching off.

Her father rubbed his eyes as if wiping away the sadness. Then he turned to Cal so suddenly, she didn't have time to look away. She faced her dad for the first time since that afternoon. The afternoon he'd smelled sweet and sour at the same time. The afternoon he'd yelled at her in a sloppy voice to get in the car to go see Mom in the hospital. The afternoon he barely avoided the tractor trailer, then skidded off the road, flipping the car and almost killing them both.

"Cal," he said. "I promise you. It won't—I won't . . . I'm going to AA in here. It's helped me a lot. And this couple comes on Sundays, and we have, like . . . church. I talk to them both a lot, and they've helped me put things in perspective. They've helped me start to forgive myself. To find my faith again and figure out—"

Cal's head popped up. *Forgive? He's* forgiven himself.

Cal didn't want to hear anymore. She wouldn't hear anymore. She wanted to tell him that he could forgive himself all he wanted. She would *never* forgive him.

Cal jumped up and ran to the door and started banging on it. "Let me out!" she shouted. "Let me out! I don't want to be here."

A corrections officer was there, followed by Cal's mom.

"Cal, stop!" Mom shouted. "What are you doing?"

"I'm going to have to escort you both out now, ma'am," the officer said. The gray steel door cranked open. Cal dashed back into the dark, dead space. She could feel her mother behind her and the corrections officer. The door slammed shut, and she jumped. Again. When she felt as if she'd explode if she didn't get out of that tiny space, the door in front of her opened. Cal darted into the waiting room, which had filled with all new sad people.

"Slow down!" an officer yelled at her.

She ran around the metal detector toward the door.

"Wait, Cal! I have to get my stuff from the locker," Mom called.

But Cal didn't wait. Soon she was outside gulping the cold, dark October air as if her throat were on fire and it was the only thing that could put out the flames.

She began to frantically rub the back of her hand.

Something about the place had made her feel as though she were covered in a layer of dirt.

After a moment, her mother walked past her. "Well, if you're in such a hurry, get in the truck already," she snapped.

Cal followed, hugging her casted arm so hard it ached.

Chapter 12

The ride home was quiet except for the music that came in and out when the radio found reception.

Now it seemed as if Mom was the one giving Cal the silent treatment, and she didn't like the role reversal at all.

As they pulled onto the highway, the radio must have found a station, because it suddenly began playing loud pop music. Just as Cal reached to shut it off, a familiar song came on, "We're Going to Dance."

The song reminded Cal of the fourth-grade Halloween party that her parents had chaperoned. Hearing it right then time-traveled her brain back to a place and time she hadn't thought about in years.

We're going to dance all day, the song droned. *Yes, we are! Then we'll dance all night!*

In her mind's eye, Cal was in the school gym. Lexi and Tonia stood in front of her, scanning the costume her mom had sewn.

"What are you?" Lexi had asked. She was dressed as Audrey from *Descendants* in a pink-and-blue wig and sparkling pink-and-black costume.

Tonia popped up next to her, looking sleek in her black-and-purple Mal costume.

Cal looked down at her own baggy cotton pants, red fabric belt, and straw hat. She'd loved the costume when Mom first showed it to her, but now it seemed drab and silly next to their shiny outfits.

"My parents and I . . . we're dressed like the characters in this book . . . that . . . ," Cal began. "Well, my dad used to read it to me." She knew it sounded babyish. "*Swiss Family Robinson.* It's about this family that gets shipwrecked on an island, and they have to survive by—"

"You look like a boy," Tonia said.

"So?" Cal turned away. She found her mother behind the food table, handing out punch. Mom didn't look drab. She was beautiful in her long dress and garland of pink and yellow flowers. Mom had wanted them to be matching, but Cal preferred the costume with pants and a feather in the hat.

Suddenly, Lexi shrieked and grabbed Tonia's arm. "Come on! They're playing 'We're Going to Dance'!"

"Oooh, I love this song!!" Tonia shouted.

The girls ran off as the entire gym seemed to erupt in dance.

We're going to dance all day. Yes, we are! Then we'll dance all night!

Cal backed into a corner to watch her classmates. It wasn't that it didn't look fun. She just didn't understand when they'd learned how to dance.

She hugged herself and glanced at the clock, wishing its hands would move faster.

"What are you doing by yourself, honey?" Mom had swept up next to her.

Cal shrugged. "I don't know how to dance."

Mom laughed. "Neither do they. Come on." She took Cal's hand.

"No, Mom. I don't want—" But suddenly they were in the middle of the hot and sweaty crowd. Mom started doing something funky with her feet as she waved her arms in the air and threw her head back.

Cal's feet remained planted. "You look ridiculous!" she shouted over the music.

Mom laughed. "I know! It's fun! You should try it!" She grabbed Cal's hands and swung her around and around. Cal couldn't help but smile . . . on the inside anyway.

"Hey! I want to join in!" Dad grabbed both of their hands. Cal couldn't stop laughing as her parents took turns spinning her in dizzying circles. When that song ended, they danced to the next one . . . and the one after that.

Later that night, Mom sat on the edge of Cal's bed. "Did you have fun?" she'd asked.

Cal nodded, still smiling on the inside.

"You really are quite the dancer," Mom said, raising an eyebrow.

Cal rolled her eyes.

"Well, I had a blast," Mom said. "Would it be okay if I chaperone the next dance too?"

Cal nodded again, but this time she smiled on the outside.

"Totally," she said.

A soft beeping noise brought Cal back to the truck's cab. The sound was coming from her mom's arm.

"What's that?" Cal asked.

Her mother pointed to the box taped to her biceps. "It's the shot of medicine I get the day after chemo. The beep is telling me that it's about to release."

"That thing is giving you a shot? Right now?"

"Yup."

"Does it hurt?"

Her mother shrugged. "A pinch."

"What does the medicine do?"

"It helps my body fight infection. Remember how I had to go to the hospital in August because I had, like . . . no white blood cells?"

Of course Cal remembered. She and Dad were on their way to see Mom when the accident happened.

"Well, this is supposed to prevent that."

Cal studied her mother's profile, then exhaled deeply, surprised at how much air she'd been holding in her lungs. She could feel some of her anger exit with it. "I'm really sorry, Mom," she finally said.

"It's not me you need to apologize to," her mother whispered.

In those words Cal could feel some of Mom's anger evaporate too.

"You need to learn to control your temper, honey." Mom seemed to shift uncomfortably in her seat.

"Are you in a lot of pain?" Cal asked.

"I'm okay."

"Does the cancer hurt?" It was something Cal had wanted to ask her mom for a long time.

"No, the cancer itself doesn't hurt, but sometimes it presses against nerves, and I can feel that."

"But that's what the chemo's fixing, right? It's making the cancer go away."

Mom took a deep breath. "That's what we need to talk about, Cal. I was going to wait, but . . ." She cleared her throat.

Cal looked out the window as trees flashed past. *No,* she thought. *No. No. No.* She'd almost convinced herself she'd made a mistake yesterday and had misunderstood the conversation between her mom and Mrs. Demsky. "You told me the chemo would make you better. You said it was like medicine, and everything would go back to normal soon."

Her mom opened her mouth as if she was going to respond, then closed it. After a moment, she said, "Well, things have changed."

Cal stared at her hands.

"In fact," Mom continued, "we need to be prepared for it to not work."

"I—I don't know what you mean," Cal said, even though she did.

"One of my doctors wanted me to have a surgery—to take out the cancer."

Cal took a big breath. "Right. Good. So, then everything will be okay."

"The problem is that the rest of the team thinks it's too risky," Mom said.

"But they'll do it, right?"

"It's up in the air."

"What does that mean? What happens if you don't get the surgery?"

Her mom lifted her chin. "That's why we've petitioned the Department of Corrections for Dad to come home early. That's what I was telling him about when I said we were supposed to hear something later today."

Cal shook her head. "What's that got to do with anything?"

"I . . . we . . . need Dad home. We have to be prepared for things to get worse."

"No," Cal said.

Mom sighed. "No what, Cal?"

"No. I don't want things to get worse, and no, I don't want him to come home."

"Unfortunately, life doesn't work like that." Mom took a deep breath. "Dad suffers from a disease like I do, Cal. I know it seems different, but alcoholism is a disease."

Cal sat up. "You didn't choose to get cancer. Dad chose

to drink too much, and then he chose to make me get in the car when he had no right driving."

"Fair enough. And he went to prison for it. But, Cal"—her mom glanced at her as if to make sure she was listening—"he's trying, and I believe him when he says it won't happen again."

Cal wanted to press her hands against her ears. She didn't want to hear any of this. But she'd known too. Even before she overheard Mom talking to Mrs. Demsky. She wished Mom had been straight with her sooner. It wouldn't change anything, but somehow Mom acting as though Cal couldn't handle the truth made her feel like she really couldn't.

Mom kept talking. "We need him home, Cal . . . in case I can't be."

Cal wanted to open the truck's door and jump out. Suddenly she felt as unsafe as she did the day of the accident, when her father kept crossing the middle lane and she wanted to grab the wheel or slam on the brake but couldn't.

"Why can't Aunt Viola help? She stayed with us when you first got sick. Why can't she come back?"

"Viola has her own family to take care of." Mom sighed. "But she did call to invite you to her house anytime. She said that even if I can't drive, you can take the bus to Manchester."

Cal didn't want to go to Viola's. She wanted to stay in her own home with her own mother.

"What about Grandpa and Grandma Scott?" Cal already knew Mom had dismissed this idea, but she had to ask again. "They took care of me when you and Dad went camping in Maine."

"That was seven years ago." Mom shook her head. "They're all the way in Florida now. Plus, I think you'd end up taking care of them."

Cal crossed her arms. "Well, I don't want him home."

"You're twelve years old, Cal. You don't understand how the world works. And you're being selfish."

"Me! Selfish?" She wanted to tell Mom about the looks. The ones she got every day at school that said everything without actually saying a word. Looks that seemed to shout, *There goes weird Cal with the weird family. There goes poor Cal Scott, whose father almost killed her and whose mother has cancer.* She thought back to the snide comments the Bee Girls whispered loud enough for her to hear: *thief, liar, pathetic.*

The radio seemed to lose the station again. Static crackled over its speakers.

Cal glanced sideways at her mother. She was biting her lip as if to keep from crying.

Tears poked at the corners of Cal's eyes too.

After a moment, Mom snapped off the radio. "He has a disease, Cal, but he's getting help now, and he'll keep doing that when he gets home. He won't even be able to drive again for a long time—the state took his license." She paused. "The truth is . . . I can't do this. I need him." She pulled on her earlobe. "And so do you."

Cal stared hard at her mother's profile. The way her cheeks sunk in and her collarbone jutted out. Cal knew she was hurting. "When?"

"We're waiting to hear. Hopefully soon."

Cal swallowed hard. "What if he drinks? What if it happens again? What will you do?"

"It won't."

"What if it does?" Cal turned to look at her mother and saw that tears had welled in her eyes.

But Mom let the question hang in the air, heavy as a rock.

Eventually her mother turned onto Main Street, then Mountain Road. As they passed the now dark market, Cal felt a tingle run up her spine. She wondered if Mr. Demsky would tell Mom about the sardines. The whole episode gave her an uneasy feeling. The old man himself made her nervous. But she was drawn to him just the same. Drawn to his stories of mountains and magic and space rocks falling to earth.

When you believe . . . that's when the impossible becomes possible. That's when you'll find the magic.

If there was anything Cal needed right then, it was to make the impossible possible.

As they turned into the driveway of their small dark home, the shadow of Mount Meteorite fell over them. Suddenly, Cal sat up. Because the universe seemed to finally be answering her. Right then, she knew what their visit to Dad had really been. A sign.

Cal raised her chin, giving the mountain a nod.

She was ready.

In the early dawn hours of the next morning, Cal threw off her covers and dressed quickly in her jeans and Lexi's pink sweatshirt. She grabbed her backpack, making sure the shoes and harnesses she'd "borrowed" from gym were still in it.

She crept down the hallway, past her mother's bedroom. In the kitchen, she scribbled out a note and left it on the table where her mother would be sure to find it.

Rummaging through a drawer, she found her father's climbing go-bag. She knew it would have important tools she might not have already stashed at the cave. She slung it across her body like a sash.

Her father's water bottle would be important since it also acted as a purifier. She grabbed that and filled it to the brim before tucking it in her side pocket. Then she opened the food cupboard, searching for anything edible. She planned to be home by dark but knew she should be ready in case things took longer. She grabbed a half loaf of bread and two granola bars. She remembered there were some cans of beans at the cave. She'd bring those too.

At the front door, she slipped into her boots. As she did, she heard a murmuring sound come from her mother's room. She walked back, gently opening the door. She peeked inside, but Mom was sound asleep, buried under her fluffy white comforter.

Suddenly Cal had such longing. She wanted to take off her heavy boots and climb into her mother's bed like she used to do when she was little and had a nightmare. She'd stand in that very doorway without making a sound. Almost immediately Mom would pop up—as if their thoughts and feelings were connected. Without waiting for Cal to explain why she was there, Mom would draw back the covers and say, *Hop in, baby. It was only a bad dream.*

Then Cal would snuggle between her parents' warm bodies. Her mom would kiss her on the forehead and say, *No more nightmares*, and Cal would drift back to sleep, knowing everything would be okay.

That was before.

Now her mother did not wake, and Cal knew that was because the cancer, or prison, or life in general, had broken their connection.

Mom was not the mother she used to be—not since the cancer, not since the accident. The magic of their relationship seemed to have disappeared so much that her mother couldn't even look her straight in the eye anymore. Somewhere deep inside, Cal knew that was because Mom was afraid that if she did, Cal would discover the truth. Her own mother couldn't keep her safe.

Tears poked at the corners of Cal's eyes. With the back of her hand, she fiercely wiped them away. At that moment she was even more confident that she was doing the right thing.

"I'm going to find the meteorite, Mom," she whispered. "I'm going to bring back our magic."

Chapter 13

Cal ran.

Up Mountain Road, past the Demskys' dark house. The sun, still hidden below the horizon, had abandoned Bleakerville to its lonely darkness. That was okay with Cal. She didn't need light to know where she was going. She was her own compass.

She pumped her fist in the air. She wanted to let the magic meteorite know she was on her way. *I'm doing it!* she wanted to shout. *I'm doing it!*

As she came to the carriage house, she veered left, making her way down the stone path. She stood facing the front door, hugging her cast. As anxious as Cal was to start her journey, she knew she couldn't do it without Rosine.

If I knock, I might wake Mali. She shook her head. *Maybe I could sneak inside?* She shook her head. *No, that could wake Mali too.*

The world was turning a lighter shade of gray. She reached for the front latch as the door flew open.

Cal jumped back in surprise.

Rosine stood in front of her wearing a nightgown. She rubbed her eyes.

"Cal?"

"Hey!" Cal whispered. "I came to get you. Let's go!"

"To school? I thought today was Saturday."

"No . . . yeah . . . today is Saturday. Not to school . . . to Mount Meteorite!" She almost giggled as the words spilled out. "I'm ready to climb the spire, and you said you wanted to do it together!"

Rosine blinked. "What time is it?"

"I don't know. Early."

Rosine hugged herself. "Can't we go later?"

"You're the one who's been begging me to do it." She shook her head. "We have to go now if we're going to make it up and back before dark." Cal frowned. "Please, Rosine. It's really important."

Rosine stared at her bare feet. Then nodded. "Okay, wait in the road for me." She ducked inside, shutting the door gently behind her.

Cal felt like doing a jig. It was working. All of her mapping and planning and plotting was finally paying off!

Soon Rosine came out dressed in jeans and her green hoodie. Her purple backpack was slung over her shoulder, and she wore the boots from the cave.

"How do they fit?" Cal asked.

"Perfect," Rosine said. "I think we're the same size."

"Of course we are!" Cal nodded. "Just wait. I have another surprise when we get to the cave. Come on, we have to go there first to feed Wildcat and grab more supplies."

As they reached the edge of the woods, Cal slapped the yellow sign before darting onto the trail.

We're doing it, she thought. *WE'RE DOING IT!*

Soon the girls were shimmying across the pencil-thin ridge, climbing over Wildcat's boulder, and jumping down onto the rock platform in front of the cave. Cal knelt and began emptying her backpack of the stuff she'd taken from the gym.

Rosine picked up a harness. "Where did you get these? It looks like what we used at school."

"I borrowed them."

"Ms. Adelman said it was okay?"

"Yeah. It's fine." She studied the supplies. "Okay, you should take a harness and a pair of climbing shoes. I brought granola bars, some bread, a Swiss Army knife, and a bottle of water we can share." She peeked inside her dad's go-bag. There was flint, matches, a compass, stoppers, and several rings of carabiners. "We'll need this stuff too."

She pulled out her notebook and flipped to the map that she'd made over the summer, showing the path leading to the spire.

"What's that?"

"My notes and drawings and stuff," Cal said. "I've been planning this for a while now." She pointed at the peak. "See that flat, stony part that the spire kind of grows out of?"

Rosine nodded.

"That's our destination. It's called Jacob's Landing."

"It looks like a giant hand," Rosine said.

"Yeah," Cal said. "People even call that stone overhang its fingertips."

Rosine nodded. "How long will it take to get to Jacob's Landing?" she asked.

"Not long. A few hours if we move fast. We should be able to scale the spire, find the meteorite, and get home before dark." Cal paused. "Is your sister going to be looking for you?"

"Mali and I had a big fight last night. She found a new apartment for us in a new city. She wants to move there right away." Rosine frowned. "She knows I want to be by myself when I'm angry. She won't look for me."

Cal's stomach fell. She'd been so worried about finding the magic meteorite for herself, she'd forgotten what was at stake for Rosine. "Well, we better get going, then," she said.

"What about you? Won't your parents look for you?" Rosine asked.

"I left a note that said I was going to my aunt's." Cal bit her lip. "It's Columbus Day weekend, you know, plus an in-service day, so no school until Wednesday. I've spent long weekends with Aunt Viola lots of times, so my mother will believe it. Viola lives in Manchester, and I usually take the bus to her house." Cal sniffed. "Mom will probably be happy I went. Anyway, by the time she figures out I'm not there, we'll be halfway up the spire." She handed Rosine a pair of climbing shoes.

"Do I put these on now?" Rosine asked.

"No, you don't want to hike in climbing shoes. They're very tight and stiff. Your feet will hurt if you try to walk in them for too long. Also, we need to protect the soles so they stay sticky for the mountain. You'll need them when we get to the spire."

Cal flipped through her notebook until she came to the page where she'd jotted down the word from the wooden box. *Amani.* "I almost forgot about this. You know, one night I was outside the Demskys', and I swear I heard someone . . . I don't know, like, singing this word. Are you sure you don't know what it means?"

When there was no answer, Cal turned around. "Rosine?"

But she wasn't there.

Cal walked inside the cave. Rosine was on her knees feeding Wildcat sardines. He made his gurgly-purr sound as if to say, *At least someone cares about me.*

"I would have done that," Cal said, feeling a twinge of jealousy.

"It's okay. I don't mind."

Cal scratched Wildcat behind the ear, then continued to the back where the supplies were.

"We only want to take what we'll need. There are some dry socks here. Make sure you take a couple of pairs. If your socks get wet, you'll end up with blisters, and then it's game over." Cal grabbed the green thirty-meter climbing rope, thought about it, then grabbed the red seventy-meter one as well. *Always have a backup*, her father would say.

She packed socks, a few tin cups, eating utensils, two cans of beans, slings, quickdraws, carabiners, two ATC belay devices, chalk bags, and a few cans of sardines. She saw a pair of tin snips she'd brought on an earlier trip. *Definitely need these*, she thought as she tucked them in her backpack.

Then she walked over to the flat rock where she'd last seen the wooden box.

The rock was empty.

She dug out her flashlight and flicked it on, directing its beam around the area.

"Did you see a wooden box here?" she asked.

Rosine was cleaning burrs from Wildcat's fur and didn't seem to hear her.

Cal stood, staring at the empty space. "It was right here," she said louder. "It was shaped like a half-moon, and it had . . . well, it had a piece of cloth inside."

I know I didn't imagine it. Cal scratched her head.

"What are these?" Rosine now stood over the pile of supplies and was holding a silver ring with a series of different-sized colorful metal pieces attached to it.

Cal frowned. An important clue was missing, and Rosine didn't seem to care.

She walked over to her and took the carabiner from her hand. "These are called passive protection pieces." She held one up. It looked like a small red wedge with about seven inches of wire threaded through it. "As we climb, I'll shove the stopper into a crack so that it wedges into the rock. Then we'll clip into the wire loop on the end with a quickdraw, which is two carabiners on each end of a piece of webbing. Then we'll thread our rope through the bottom carabiner of the draw. I keep placing the protection pieces in the rock along the way, so that if I slip while climbing, you stop me from falling, and same when you climb."

"Hmmm." Rosine stared hard at Cal. "I didn't want to ask before, but how are you going to climb with that thing on your arm?"

"My cast?" Cal shook her head. "I know what I'm doing."

Rosine raised her eyebrows. "Okay."

Cal shined her flashlight one more time around the cave. The box seemed to have vanished as mysteriously as it had appeared.

Rosine hitched her purple backpack on her back. "Ready?" she asked.

Cal nodded, trying to forget about the box and the funny feeling she had that Rosine knew more than she was sharing. "Okay, let's go."

The girls exited the cave and shimmied across the ridge, Wildcat behind them.

"Is this safe for him?" Rosine asked.

"Of course," Cal replied. "The mountain is his home. The first time I met him, he was scurrying across this ridge. That's how I found the cave." The memory made her smile on the inside. "When I made it to his boulder, he looked up at me, and I swear I heard him say, *Okay, we can be friends, but next time bring food.*"

Rosine grinned.

"Sardines are his favorites. We spent most of the summer and early fall exploring. Sometimes he disappears for a couple days, but he always finds me. Right, Wildcat?"

Wildcat made a grumbly sound as if to say, *Less chit-chat. More focus!*

The girls laughed as they hopped onto the path.

"How's the backpack feel?" Cal asked.

Rosine lifted her chin. "This is nothing."

"Good," Cal said. "We have a long way to go."

Chapter 14

As they marched on, Cal couldn't get the image of the wooden box and the word stitched in green and gold out of her mind. She thought back to the last time she'd been in the cave, two days ago. Was it there then? She'd been so distracted by the lateness of the day and the fact that Rosine had unexpectedly shown up, she'd forgotten to look for it.

Cal had a hard time believing Rosine would take something that wasn't hers. She'd seemed upset about the climbing shoes and the harnesses. Still, a feeling kept nagging at her that Rosine knew more than she was telling. *Maybe she took it, and now she's afraid to admit it?* Cal shook her head. If the word really was a clue that could lead them to the meteorite, she needed to find out soon. If Rosine wasn't going to confess, the only thing left to do would be to peek inside her purple backpack when she wasn't looking.

Suddenly, both girls froze. In front of them stood a massive oak, split straight down the middle. Although the left and right sides had fallen away from each other, the base was still held together by a shared trunk and roots. It looked like a giant uppercase *V*.

"Whoa," Cal said. "What happened to the tree?"

"Ni umeme did this," Rosine said. "I don't know how to say it in English. You know, when there is a flash of light in the sky?"

"Oh, you mean lightning. Yeah, you're right. A lightning bolt must have hit the tree. It wasn't like that last time I was here." Cal studied Rosine. "What did you just call the lightning?"

"Umeme," Rosine said.

"Umeme," Cal repeated. "I like that."

Out of nowhere, Wildcat leapt into the middle of the tree.

Rosine gasped. "That cat is like a ghost. He disappears and then appears out of nowhere. *Poof!*"

"Wildcat is stealthy," Cal said. "And smart." She glanced around. Everything looked so different than it had when she'd first started exploring. In July and August, the leaves were lush and green. In September, they'd turned a sunny yellow. Now, in October, some had already turned brown and many had fallen away, concealing the path she'd forged in earlier months.

"Are we lost?" Rosine asked.

Cal shook her head. "I know where I'm going." She slowly turned in a circle, then pointed to the right. "This way," she finally said.

Rosine followed.

"What language were you speaking?" Cal asked. "You know, when you said that word . . . *umeme*?"

"That's Swahili—my first language. I also speak Kirundi and French."

"Because you are from Congo, right? Where is that again?"

"Central Africa. There are actually two countries called Congo—the Republic of Congo, which is also called Congo-Brazzaville, and Democratic Republic of Congo, where I'm from, called DRC or Congo-Kinshasa. But like I told you, there was a war and we had to leave."

"What was that like?"

"I can remember being in a crowded boat. It was like a hollowed-out log. We crossed Lake Tanganyika into Burundi in that skinny boat."

"You and your sister, Mali?"

"Oh no, it was all of us then. My mother and father. And my grandmother." Rosine paused. "There were five of us once," she whispered.

Cal was pretty sure Rosine's parents had died. She wasn't sure what had happened to the rest of her family, but she felt uncomfortable asking.

"It got better, though, right? I mean, after you escaped the war?"

"People think that when you escape one bad situation, everything will suddenly be perfect. But I have found that is never the case. When we came to Burundi, we were refugees. We had no money, and my father couldn't find work. There were other problems too."

"Like what?"

Rosine was quiet, then said, "People have tried to treat me like an outsider for as long as I can remember. When you are a little kid, you accept it. You think, *Well, I must be less than them. These adults understand the world better than me, and I must not be as good because I am small or because I don't know the language or because I am . . . different somehow.*"

Cal thought about that. Even though she'd lived in Bleakerville her whole life, she felt as if she were different too. It was as if all the other kids spoke some secret language, and no matter how hard she tried, she couldn't figure it out.

She knew that her experiences weren't anything like Rosine's. She would never know what that was like. Still, she knew how it felt to be on the outside looking in. She thought back to the first day she met Rosine. The new girl had smiled at her and saved her a seat on the bus ride home. But Cal had simply turned away. Even though Cal hadn't done anything mean, wasn't ignoring her the same as saying, *You are an outsider*? And didn't that make her as guilty as the Bee Girls?

Cal bit her lip, embarrassed by how she'd acted. She glanced at Rosine, suddenly wanting everything to be different for her in Bleakerville.

"Things are better now, though, aren't they? You know, here in the United States . . . there's, like, a better life . . . and, you know, freedom and stuff?"

"Yes and no. I don't think any one person deserves more rights or opportunities than another, no matter where they live, do you?"

"Um, well, no. Of course not."

"I'm treated like an outsider here too, you know. I do my best to ignore it. Still, I dress differently. I definitely talk differently." She shrugged. "Mali and I have been here for over a year, and that has changed my thinking.

Now I know that the *better life* you talk about isn't going to come from *where* I live. It's going to come from *who* I am—who I choose to be." She lifted her chin. "So . . . here in Bleakerville . . . I have chosen to be me. Rosine Kanambe!"

Cal looked at Rosine, in awe of her confidence. Still, she knew from experience that wasn't as easy as Rosine made it sound. Saying you weren't going to let something bother you didn't make the hurt go away.

"Is that kind of why you want to find the magic too? To give you . . . I don't know . . . like, the strength or power or whatever to do that?"

Rosine paused. "Yes," she finally said. "Definitely."

"Okay," Cal said. "Well, let's get to it, then."

After about a half hour of more hiking, Cal was beginning to wonder if they were heading in the wrong direction. She paused, trying to get her bearings.

"Are we lost?" Rosine asked.

"Um, I'm not sure." The sound of rushing water gave her a reason to find out. "Let's take a break and hydrate while I check my map."

At the stream's bank, Cal removed her backpack and dug out the bottle of water. "I brought this for us to share." She handed it to Rosine, who took a sip, then handed it back.

"It's okay, you should drink more," Cal said. "I can refill it." She dug out her notebook and studied the map she'd drawn of the path from the cave to Jacob's Landing. She shook her head, realizing they should have turned left at the oak that had been split by lightning, not right. She opened her dad's compass and reoriented, quickly confirming that they'd just wasted an hour hiking in the wrong direction.

Rosine gave Cal the bottle. She drank what was left, then knelt by the stream, lowering it into the rapidly running water.

"We can drink that water? Isn't it dirty?" Rosine asked.

"This is a special bottle. It filters out bacteria, like giardia, that will make you sick if—"

A squeal from Rosine almost sent Cal tumbling into the stream.

Rosine pointed. "What is that creature?"

"What?" Cal looked up.

There, sauntering toward them, was a giant black bear. Cal dropped the bottle. "It—it's okay." She scrambled backward. "It's scared of us too. GO!" she shouted. "Go away! We need to yell at him!"

Rosine didn't budge.

Cal slowly retreated, linking arms with her. "This will make us look bigger. Wave at him and shout!"

Rosine came to life, waving her arms. "Ondoka! Ondoka!" she shouted.

Together, the girls inched backward as the bear lumbered to where Cal had been standing. He picked up the water bottle and tried to bite it. When he realized it wasn't food, he let it fall into the current, where it floated away. Then he turned his attention to Cal's backpack.

"Our food," Cal whispered as the bear buried his nose inside the bag.

Obviously sniffing something good, he pulled out a granola bar. When he finished that, he started in on the bread.

"Wildcat!" Cal's heart dropped as she watched the cat creep toward the bear. "No! Come!"

Wildcat didn't listen. Instead, he skulked closer to the bear, whose muzzle was again buried inside the backpack. When the bear finally lifted his snout, he seemed surprised to see a black ball of fur hissing at him.

The bear dropped the backpack, letting it fall into the water. He growled at the cat and showed his sharp white teeth.

The girls jumped back, but Wildcat stood his ground. The bear extended his nose as if to sniff at the cat. Wildcat lifted a paw, swatting it. Dots of blood dripped from the bear's nose. He made a moaning sound, probably wondering how something so small could hurt so much.

Done with the cat and the backpack, the bear lumbered to the far bank. Wildcat scrambled over the rocks, chasing after him.

Cal rushed into the stream. "No! Come back, Wildcat!"

But the bear and the cat were gone.

Cal bent down and lifted the drenched backpack. Water poured from it. She looked downstream for the water bottle, but it was gone along with the bread and granola bars.

"Great." She climbed out, her feet sloshing with each step. "This," she said, "is a problem."

"The food?"

"No. My feet. I can't hike in wet boots." Cal blinked hard. It wasn't noon yet, and everything was going wrong.

"Are you sure you can't hike in the climbing shoes?"

Cal shook her head.

Rosine sat down and began unlacing a boot.

"What are you doing?"

"I'm not waiting for that bear to come back." She handed Cal a sock and a boot. "If we each wear one, we'll be the same."

Cal looked at the boot, then Rosine. "You would do that for me?"

"They *are* yours," Rosine said matter-of-factly.

"Did you grab the extra socks?"

Rosine opened her pack and dug out a dry pair. She handed them to Cal.

When they each had a stockinged foot and a booted foot, Cal said, "Okay. Um . . . here's the thing." She pointed in the direction they'd come. "Turns out we were supposed to be going that way."

"We're lost?"

"We were, but now I know the right way."

"Are you sure?"

Cal nodded.

Rosine sighed. "Let's go, then."

Cal was relieved Rosine wasn't mad.

"What about Wildcat?" Rosine asked.

"He's okay," Cal said. "He'll find me. He always does."

Chapter 15

The girls tossed on their backpacks. Cal's dripped, but the cool damp felt good. They moved slowly, careful to avoid rocks and sticks. When they finally got back to the giant V-shaped oak, Cal double-checked her map, and they continued in what she now knew was the right direction.

The adrenaline from the bear encounter made her forget about her thirst for a while, but after another hour of hiking, Cal's mouth began to feel like sandpaper again. She didn't want to stop and figure it out. She was anxious to keep moving. Maybe if they found another stream, she could boil the water to purify it. But she knew the mountain well enough to know there weren't any streams near Jacob's Landing.

"What's the matter?" Rosine asked.

"What?"

"You're shaking your head. What's wrong?"

"Water," Cal said. "We need to find drinkable water."

"Oh, that. I can take care of that."

"How?"

"I'll show you when we get there."

Cal rolled her eyes. "There isn't any water at the top."

"Are there trees?"

"Yeah, not on Jacob's Landing itself—that's all rock—but around it."

Just as they were about to emerge from the forest, they paused. There, in front of them, was an enormous ash tree that appeared as if it had been pulled straight out of the ground. It lay on its side, leaving a massive hole in the earth where its root ball had once been. The tree's long, wiry roots now dangled across the front entrance to this underground cave like a beaded-string curtain.

"What did that?" Rosine asked.

"A storm, I guess. It must have rained hard, loosening the soil, and then a strong wind knocked the tree over."

"It looks as if kiumbe kikubway has come here and

pulled the tree out by its roots." Rosine leaned forward, adjusting the root curtain and peeking inside. "It's big enough in there to be someone's house."

Cal had seen this ash tree before. A few years ago, she and her dad had come across it while hiking to the landing.

Always be careful near fallen trees, he'd told Cal. *Sometimes they can pop back into place.* He'd walked around the ash, examining it. *This one's secure, though*, he continued. *See how its trunk is entrenched in the landscape? It's been here for years. It's not going anywhere.*

Cal had ducked inside the dirt cave, peeking back out through the roots to make her dad laugh.

She shook away the memory. "I wouldn't get so close," she said to Rosine. "Someone might already be living there."

Rosine jumped back.

"Come on," Cal said. "We're almost at the landing. Let's go."

The girls emerged from the forest onto a large, flat granite area that looked like an enormous stone balcony. Immediately the wind picked up, tousling Cal's already messy hair. She breathed in the clean mountain air and sighed.

"Welcome to Jacob's Landing," she said. The sight of the spire still took her breath away.

They walked across the smooth stone until they stood at the spire's base.

Rosine raised her chin, staring straight up. Clouds scudded across the spire's peak. "So that's it, huh?"

Cal stood next to her. "Yup."

"Looks even taller from here."

Cal opened her mouth to say something but didn't trust her own voice. The spire appeared the way Mr. Lopez described: smooth as glass. She hugged her casted arm.

"Unless you've got a magic elevator in your backpack, I don't know how you're going to get up there with one arm," Rosine said.

Cal looked at the sun, which seemed to be lowering faster than it was supposed to. She knew they weren't going to have enough time to scale the spire, find the meteorite, and get back before dark. A reality was starting to set in. She tried to swallow. Her tongue felt thick, her throat dry.

"I don't know, Rosine," Cal said.

"What do you mean?"

"It took longer to get here than it was supposed to, and we have no water." She bit her lip.

"I told you, I will take care of that, but I'll need your red knife and a bowl."

Cal lowered her backpack and dug through it until

she found her Swiss Army knife and an aluminum cup. She handed them to Rosine, wondering how these things were going to help find water.

Still wearing only one boot, Rosine walked unevenly into the forest.

Cal followed.

Rosine pointed to a long vine, as thick as her arm, that was wrapped around an oak. "This is all over the woods. Do you know what it is?"

Cal examined it. "Yes. My dad taught me about plants in case I ever got lost on one of our hikes. It's a wild grapevine."

Rosine scraped away a section of the vine and then punctured it with the point of the knife. She put the tin cup on the ground under that spot. Then she moved to the other end and pierced another hole. Soon they heard the *plunk, plunk, plunk* of water drops falling into the cup.

"It will take a while," Rosine said. "But we will have water."

"The vine acts like a purifier?" Cal asked.

"Yes. It will be good water."

Cal raised her eyebrows in admiration. "Wow! That's so cool," she said. "Where did you learn that?"

"I know how to take care of myself. Are you ready to climb?" Rosine said as she headed back to the landing.

When they were back at the spire's base, Cal shaded her eyes as she focused on the horizon. "The other problem is that even though we probably have enough daylight to get up the spire, it will be too dark to get back down." She hugged her casted arm—which was the third problem she didn't want to mention. She'd had a plan to take care of her cast, but like everything else, there wasn't enough time.

"We came so far." Rosine looked at the spire, then the path they'd emerged from, then back at the peak. "What if we stayed here tonight and climbed early tomorrow morning?" she asked.

The sun hung low in the sky.

"Won't Mali come looking for you?"

"I told you. We got in a fight. Mali is stubborn, but she thinks I'm more stubborn. She will not look for me."

Rosine's determination shifted something inside Cal.

"You're right, Rosine. We should camp here tonight."

"Your family won't look for you?" Rosine asked.

"My mom will be worried when she finds out I'm not at Viola's." She shook off a twinge of guilt. "But if we start tomorrow at dawn, we can be home by noon, so it will be okay." Cal nodded. "Let's set up camp there." She pointed to a spot in the middle of the landing. "And make a fire here. It's totally safe on the ledge."

"Yes!" Rosine grinned. "But what are we using to make a shelter?"

"Branches and leaves and sticks. Grab what you can find that's fallen in the woods, and then I'll show you how to make a lean-to."

"Did your father teach you this too?" Rosine asked.

"I guess." Cal ducked into the woods and came back with a branch slightly taller than she was. "This is what we want," she said, showing it to Rosine. "See how it has kind of a *V* on the end? Help me find more branches like this one."

Soon the girls had collected a stack. "We need to fix these three tall branches so that all the *V*'s intersect in a tripod. That's our frame," she said. "Now add more branches all around it to make sides. Don't forget to leave a space for a doorway."

When they finished, Cal said, "We're not done yet." She ducked into the woods and returned with an armful of debris. "If we cover it with moss and leaves and stuff, it'll be waterproof and keep us warm."

Rosine followed, and they layered their stick frame with leaves and brush until their shelter looked like part of the landscape.

Even though Cal was nervous about staying on the mountain overnight, there was something exciting about creating this place with Rosine. It was as if they were the real Swiss Family Robinson on an adventure.

Cal held up a can of baked beans. "Now, how about a fire so we can warm these up?" She arranged rocks in a large circle in the middle of the landing. When she finished, they collected dried leaves, twigs, and branches, and she separated them into piles by size. She dug through her backpack and pulled out the matches. Wet. "These are worthless." She threw them on the ground.

She stared at the can of beans.

"It's okay, we can eat them cold," Rosine said.

"They'll taste better hot," Cal said. "Plus, it's going to get really cold as soon as the sun goes down." She found her dad's go-bag and dug out the flint. She'd never started a fire from friction, but she'd seen him do it. "We need more tinder."

"What's that?"

"Stuff that's super combustible and will light easily." She squinted, scanning the forest. "Birch bark," she said. "See that white tree that fell over there? Can you bring me some of the bark from the dead part?"

As Rosine headed back into the woods, Cal found a piece of hard quartz.

"Is this right?" Rosine asked, showing a stack of bark as thin as paper.

"Perfect." Then Cal remembered another trick her dad had taught her. "Is your sock inside your boot still dry?"

Rosine nodded.

"Take it off," Cal said as she removed hers. "See these tiny pills on our socks? We need to pick them all off and make a pile."

Rosine's forehead wrinkled, but she did it.

When that was done, Cal placed the birch bark in the center and the sock fuzz on top of that. She struck the quartz against the flint in short, quick motions. Sparks flew. Cal kept at it, aiming the shower of sparks at the mound of sock fuzz. Soon, it began to smoke and a tiny flame erupted. Cal blew gently until it caught on the birch bark. She added the smallest twigs, eventually adding bigger and bigger sticks and then branches. The fire grew, licking the air and throwing heat.

"You did it!" Rosine grinned. "I'll check on the water."

Cal grabbed two cans of beans and opened them with her Swiss Army knife. She was tucking them inside the hot coals when she saw Wildcat saunter across the landing.

"Well, look who shows up when it's dinnertime," Cal said.

Wildcat brushed against her. Cal scratched behind his ear. "Don't worry, I brought some food for you."

Soon Rosine was back. "Hey, Wildcat found us," she said.

"I told you he would," Cal said, freeing a twig from his fur.

Rosine handed her the cup. It was filled to the brim.

"Wow. There was a lot of water in that vine."

When she thought the beans were warm enough, she used a stick to remove the cans. "Careful—it will burn you." She handed Rosine a spoon. Soon they were kneeling over their cans and eating a hot dinner.

The girls took turns sipping the water. "It tastes grape flavored," Cal said. When they'd both had enough to drink, she put the cup down for Wildcat, who lapped up the rest, then meowed as if to say, *Not bad.*

Rosine laughed as Wildcat curled up between them.

"I forgot to tell you, I packed dessert." Rosine dug into her backpack and pulled out a Snickers bar. As she did, a small glass jar fell out.

"What's that?" Cal asked as Rosine put the jar back in her bag.

"Oh," Rosine said. "Do you need it?"

Cal shook her head. "No, but why did you bring it?"

Rosine shrugged. "It's something I do. I take some dirt from places I want to remember."

Cal nodded, but she didn't really understand. She'd lived in the same place her whole life and wasn't sure how saving dirt in a jar would help her remember anything.

Rosine pointed upward. The sun was beginning to hit the peak of the spire.

Maybe it was because they were sitting directly below it, but it seemed to explode in light more brilliant than anything she'd ever seen. Bright as a second sun. Cal felt as if the spire were shining just for them.

That's when Cal heard a sniff. She turned to see Rosine wipe away a tear.

"You believe there's magic up there too don't you?" Cal whispered.

"One hundred percent sure." Rosine said.

Wildcat made his gurgly-purr sound.

"See? Even he likes it," Cal said.

Rosine laughed.

As the fire crackled, the girls enjoyed their candy bar. When they finished, Rosine placed several small round rocks in the coals.

"What are you doing?" Cal asked.

"When these are hot, we'll put them inside your wet boots to help them dry faster."

"Oh yeah?" Cal said. "That's a good idea."

Cal wiped out the bean cans as best she could. "Can we make holes in more vines to get more water?"

"Sure," Rosine said. "I'll do it now."

Cal wondered if Rosine would leave her backpack behind, but she tossed it over her shoulder as usual. When she returned, Cal was sitting by the fire holding scissors.

"What are those?" Rosine asked.

"Tin snips."

"What are you doing with them?"

"Not me. You."

Rosine sat next to her. "Okay. What am I doing with them?"

Cal held out her casted arm. "You are going to cut this off."

"Your arm?"

"Ha ha, very funny." Cal rolled her eyes. "My cast."

Rosine's forehead wrinkled.

"It's ready . . . my arm, I mean. I'm supposed to get the cast off on Monday. A couple days early won't matter. And I've seen it done on YouTube. It's not easy, but you're strong."

Rosine shook her head. "What if I hurt you?"

"You won't. Start by making little cuts. If we keep at it, I'll eventually be able to peel it off."

Rosine knelt next to Cal. She began cutting the plaster in small bites. "This is going to take forever."

"Keep going. You're getting it."

"It's hard." Rosine made an *umphh* noise with each snip. Soon she was halfway up Cal's forearm. She shook her hand out. "I need to rest."

"Okay." Cal pulled at the cast. "Ahhh . . . this already feels so much better."

Soon Rosine started in again, cutting the rest away.

Cal pulled at the plaster as if it were a pea pod. When it was wide enough, she slipped her arm out. "Hand me the snips." She cut away the gauze her arm was wrapped in.

"Finally!" she said when they finished. Her skin was pink and shriveled. She rubbed it with her right hand. "I have waited so long to do this!" She moved her arm, bending her elbow, then looked at Rosine. "Thank you."

Rosine shook her head. "I've never met anyone like you, Cal."

Cal grinned. "I've never met anyone like you." She leaned back against a rock. "Check it out," she said, pointing at the sky. Red, orange, yellow, blue, and violet streaks stacked like pancakes across the horizon. Each color blurred into the next. Cal inhaled deeply as if breathing in the colors. She closed her eyes and sighed, feeling the night wrap around her like a warm hug.

As the colors faded and the fire crackled, Cal looked around the landing. In one day, they'd hiked most of the mountain, escaped a bear, found water, built a shelter, made a fire, and freed her casted arm.

She turned her gaze to the spire. It seemed to rise like a monument against the rainbow sky.

Cal gave it a nod. *You're next.*

Chapter 16

As the sun disappeared below the horizon, Cal felt the darkness creep over them. She pulled down the sleeves of her pink sweatshirt and shivered. "We better hit the sack."

"Why would we hit our sack?"

"It's an expression. It means go to sleep."

"Oh."

Cal smothered the last embers of the fire. Wildcat stirred and stretched, then curled back in his furry ball as the girls crawled inside their stick-and-leaf shelter.

It felt as if they were sleeping inside the mountain itself.

"I want to keep my head outside," Rosine said. "So we can look at the stars."

"Okay, I guess."

They dug their heels into the ground, scooting their bodies forward until their heads popped out.

Stars were scattered like silver confetti across the sky.

"Sometimes Mali and I would stay out all night. We'd fall asleep leaning against each other."

"Tell me more about where you grew up. Tell me about something you miss."

"I miss my friends." Rosine sighed. "In Burundi, I played a lot of jump rope with my girlfriends. Sometimes the mothers would join us. Then it would get dark and they would go home, but we would keep going." She continued, "My favorite is soccer, though."

"You like soccer?"

"I love it. There were no girls' teams so I would play with the boys. We'd play soccer all day. It would get dark, but I wouldn't come home until our match was done."

"You like to stay busy, like me."

"Yes, but it was also like this—if I kept moving, I wouldn't feel so hungry all the time."

"What do you mean?"

"You know, when there was no food—if I kept moving, it was easier to keep my mind off my empty stomach."

"Oh."

"You and I are the same, I think?" Rosine said.

"Me?" Cal shook her head. She was embarrassed to say that she'd never gone a day without eating. Even when her dad lost his job at the garage and her favorite snacks weren't in the cupboard like before, there was always something to eat.

"Yes." Rosine nodded. "You aren't trying to ignore hunger pains, but I think you are trying to ignore other pains. You run and move constantly so you won't feel them."

"That's not true," Cal said. She didn't want to talk about her feelings with Rosine . . . or anyone.

"Okay," Rosine said. "Whatever you say."

Cal decided to change the subject. "So, what were your favorite foods in Burundi?"

"All kinds of fruits. I love mango and papaya especially. One time," Rosine continued, "Mali and I were walking with Mama, and we came across some mango trees. Mama had picked one and handed it to me." Rosine closed her eyes. "Just as I went to take that first, sweet bite, Mali snatched it and ran off."

"That was mean," Cal said.

Rosine laughed. "Not really. I was teasing her with the mango. I was making sure she saw that Mama gave it to me and not her."

"Did you let Mali have it?"

"No! I raced after her. When I caught up to her, the mango was gone. She was licking the juice from her sticky fingers and laughing at me."

"She ate it without sharing?"

"Oh yeah," Rosine said. "But I didn't let her get away with it. I pulled her hair so hard. Then Mama caught up with us."

"Who got in trouble?"

"We both did." Rosine shook her head, laughing. "My mother . . . I thought she would have us by our noses. She shook her finger at us. *You are sisters first!* she said. *You must help each other. Always!*" Rosine turned away as if searching the sky for something. "You are sisters first," she repeated.

In the distance, a coyote howled, followed by the *yip, yip, yip* of its pack.

Cal studied Rosine's profile. Something seemed to have shifted inside her. It was as if her story had conjured up ghosts of a faraway place. Cal felt a tingle run up her spine.

"Well, that's what you're doing now, right? You're helping Mali by finding the magic," Cal said.

Rosine didn't answer. Cal was worried she'd upset her.

"Tell me something you say in Swahili. You know like

164

I said *hit the sack* . . . Do you have, like, a saying or something?"

"If my mother heard us complain about anything, she would say, *Maisha ni mapambano, ili upate amani utapitia mengi.*"

Until then Cal had only heard Rosine speak a few words in Swahili. But hearing her repeat her mother's familiar phrase sounded different. Her words spilled easily, blending so that Cal couldn't tell where one word began and the next ended. She wondered if that was how English had sounded to Rosine at first. Sleek and rapid.

"Wow," Cal said. "Swahili is so different but so pretty. What does that mean?"

"It translates like this—'Life is a struggle. To find peace you will have to go through a lot.'"

"I love that." Cal sighed. "That's really amazing, you know?"

"What?"

"I mean, I hadn't thought about it before, but you . . . just coming here. After everything you've been through. And then not understanding what anyone was saying." Cal shook her head. "I couldn't do it."

"Like my mother told us, it's a struggle. But that's how you find peace," Rosine said. "And you *could* do it, Cal.

You'd be surprised what you can do when you have no choice."

Cal let Rosine's words sink in.

Rosine yawned. "Maybe Mali has decided not to wait for me and she's already left for her new home without me. Maybe she doesn't care if I come or not."

Cal wondered about her own mother and if she had realized Cal never made it to Viola's. She felt a sharp jab in her heart. On the hike up, she'd occasionally glanced over her shoulder, checking to see if anyone was looking for them. And again, when they were at the landing, she scoured below for flashlights. No one was ever there.

"You know, you never told me what the magic meteorite is supposed to look like," Rosine said.

Cal had given it a lot of thought. Even though no one knew for sure, Cal had taken out books from the library. "Most meteorites look like ordinary rocks. They're usually black and often smooth or shiny. But I have a feeling that this meteorite is different."

"How?"

"I think it will glow or burn brightly; you know the way the peak looks like it's on fire when the sun hits it?"

"Yeah."

"In my head, I've always thought that must be the meteorite. To me it looks like fire on ice."

"Maybe," Rosine said. "So how did you learn to climb something as steep as the spire?"

"My dad."

"Is that where you got all this equipment?"

"Some of it," Cal said.

"Won't he notice it's missing?"

"No."

"Why not?"

Cal sighed. She could lie. She could say he didn't notice that kind of thing, or that he no longer lived at home. But something about the way Rosine had trusted her enough to share her stories—hard stories—made Cal want to tell the truth.

"He's in prison."

"Like jail prison?"

Cal ignored the question, instead scanning the sky until she found the Big Dipper. She lifted her arm, enjoying her new feeling of lightness. With her pointer finger, she followed the two outer stars of the constellation's bowl to the Little Dipper's handle and the North Star, Polaris. Another trick her dad had taught her.

"Why?" Rosine asked.

"Why what?"

"Why is he in jail prison?"

"I don't want to talk about it."

"You're mad at him for this."

Cal lowered her arm. "Of course I'm mad. He . . . He almost killed me."

"Your father tried to kill you?"

It sounded different when Rosine said it. "No. Not like that. He didn't mean to. He's an alcoholic, and he drank, and then he drove with me in the car."

"Is that how your arm got broken?"

Cal thought for a moment. "Yeah."

"That's wrong."

"Yes, it's wrong. It's awful. It's . . . I'll never forgive him for what he did."

"But it seems that he did many good things too. No? Every time I ask you questions about making a fire or where you learned how to climb, you tell me your father taught you."

Cal was getting angry. Rosine didn't understand. "Well, there's other stuff too. The shutters are falling off the house, and there's a hole punched in the wall, which is his fault too, by the way, and he's not there to fix it or help Mom or me or anything."

"He punched a hole in the wall?"

"Look, Rosine, you don't get it. He's not home like he's supposed to be. He abandoned me when I needed him most."

"My father left," Rosine said.

"What?" Cal stared at Rosine's profile. "I thought he died."

"No. My mother died. My father . . . he left us. One day he was gone, and I never saw him again."

Cal didn't understand how Rosine spoke so plainly about such painful things. It reminded Cal of what she'd said earlier—*I have chosen to be me. Rosine Kanambe.* She wasn't running from her truth.

"You are your own universe, Rosine, like Mr. Demsky said."

"Yes." She nodded. "We both are."

"Hmmm," Cal said. It was a nice thing to say, but she didn't feel that way. "I'm sorry, Rosine."

"Why are you sorry?"

"I'm sorry you've had to face so many . . . really hard things."

The girls were silent.

"So . . . how do you do that?" Cal asked. "How do you get through . . . all that stuff . . . and still . . . I don't know . . . keep going?"

"When I was in the refugee camp and it was only Mali and me, sometimes she wouldn't talk to me. I think she felt a lot of responsibility for me, and she was just a kid too. But I didn't understand that. It made me so sad. I began to feel as if I'd fallen in a deep hole. I was so far down I couldn't see the top."

"How did you get out?"

"I imagined a rope."

"A rope?"

"Yes. I imagined that someone threw me a thick rope. It was brown and rough and twisted, but in my mind, it was real and it was strong," Rosine said. "Even if I close my eyes now, I can still feel how its fibers are prickly to the touch. How they gave me something to hold on to."

"You used the rope to imagine climbing out of the hole?"

"Not right away," Rosine said. "Most days I was too tired to climb. Lots of times I felt as if I were slipping, down, down, down. We had applied for resettlement. We had many, many interviews. Each month that we heard nothing back, I felt myself sliding lower and lower. I thought the rope would end, and there would be no way out of the darkness."

"What did you do?"

"I tied a knot. In my mind I tied a knot at the very bottom of the rope. A big, thick, fat knot. Then I stood on that knot and rested. I held on and waited until I could be strong again. It is very hard in the refugee camp. At first, you are living in these tents with nothing inside. Then they give you this space to build a house, but we have no materials to make a home with. For food they gave us fufu powder, salt, some oil, and they said *go make a meal*, but it was never enough. We were always hungry." Rosine sighed. "When I couldn't face things anymore, I would feel that knot below my feet and I would tell myself, *It's okay, Rosine. That's enough for today. Rest now.*"

She continued, "From those few words, I could find the strength to hold on." She took a deep breath. "Finally, when I felt my muscles come back . . . very slowly I began to climb again. In my mind I could watch myself climb up that rope. Climb . . . rest . . . climb . . . rest . . . climb. Higher and higher until I could see a tiny bit of light. That's when we got the news. Mali and I had been selected for resettlement to the United States. We were going to America."

Cal could feel Rosine's happiness bubble out from her memory.

"It was as if the imaginary person who had thrown me the rope reached down and yanked me right out of that dark place," Rosine said.

Cal thought about that. About how with every bad thing that happened—doctors and cancer and hospitals and prison—she felt as if she were falling too. Down, down, down, with no end in sight.

"For me it's this mountain," Cal said. "When I'm here, everything changes. That's how I know there is something to Mr. Demsky's story. This place is magic. But when I have to go back to the real world . . ." She sighed. "It's like trying to grab on to water. The magic slips through my fingers, as if it were never there in the first place."

"When I was holding on to the rope, there were things I did to make myself lighter."

"Lighter?"

"Yeah. There were things weighing me down. Making me feel heavy. That was what was making me fall."

"What made you feel heavy?"

"Anger. I was angry at my father for leaving. And I was angry at my mother for getting sick."

"But it wasn't your mother's fault that she got sick."

"Yes. But I was still angry at her. She was supposed to take care of us. That was her job. I was just a kid, and I had to take care of her. I was really mad at her for that."

"So, what did you do?"

"I forgave them both."

"And then?"

"And then it got better."

Suddenly, Cal was cold. Her teeth began to chatter. The night sky didn't feel like a hug anymore, it felt as if it were closing in on her. "We need to get some sleep." As the words came out of her mouth, she was mad at herself. It was something her dad would have said.

Cal scooted her body all the way inside the shelter and rolled over so she faced the stick wall. She could hear Rosine scramble in beside her. Soon she was snoring lightly.

Cal knew she needed rest too, but no matter how magical the mountain felt during the day, she worried it couldn't protect her from the demons who invaded her dreams at night. And no matter how hard she fought it, the nightmare won.

Cal opens her eyes. Immediately she feels her body moving forward, again stuck inside the invisible current. She wriggles against it, trying to walk backward, but her feet won't budge. She twists left and right, fighting against the force, but the current holds her prisoner.

The angry mirror-person at the end of the corridor draws her in like a magnet. Faster and faster, until she's so close that if she reaches out, she'll touch its face.

The embers of anger and fear deep inside her swirl together until they form a scream that rises up through her stomach and into her throat—jabbing and poking and burning.

She opens her mouth as if to release the scream, but no sound comes out.

She tries again, opening her mouth as wide as possible.

Then, just as the scream might emerge, somewhere in the back of her brain she hears a voice.

A song.

"Amani."

Cal shot up. "What?"

In the darkness, Cal blinked, trying to remember where she was. Trying to remember why she was cold and damp. Her heart beat like a hummingbird stuck in her rib cage.

Breathe.

It took a minute for her brain to catch up with her heart.

"Okay." She inhaled the musty smell of leaves and sticks. She felt the hard earth below. "I'm here. On the mountain. I'm okay."

She squinted against the darkness, feeling for Rosine. But the space next to her was empty.

Chapter 17

Cal crawled out of their stick hut. The night air was cool and crisp. Although it felt as if she'd barely slept, she could see a thin orange line tracing the horizon. Dawn was breaking.

Cal squinted, scanning Jacob's Landing until she spotted the silhouette of a girl sitting on the edge of its "fingertips."

Cal walked toward her. "What are you doing?"

Rosine jumped a little, knocking a stone with her hand and sending it over the edge. "Don't do that! You scared me," she said in a sharp tone Cal had never heard her use.

Her purple backpack was there, and as Cal sat down, Rosine pulled it onto her lap.

Something about that made Cal mad. She wanted to ask her what she was hiding. "Why are you out here?" she asked.

"I couldn't sleep." Rosine pointed in the direction of the rock falling into the abyss below. "Not the best way down, hey?"

"Was that you before?" Cal tilted her head in a question. "Like ten minutes ago. I was . . . I was asleep, and . . . I was having this dream . . . or nightmare, I guess, and I heard singing."

Suddenly, Cal wasn't so sure. The word that woke her. *Amani.* Did it come from Rosine or her nightmare? "Was that you?" she asked again.

"I don't know what you're talking about." Rosine looked annoyed.

Cal studied her profile.

"It's kind of scary here. But very peaceful too. I can almost pretend I am back in Burundi," Rosine said. "This is something Mali and I would have done on the mountain near the camp. We'd look down below and watch the kids lining up for school. We'd say to each other, *Someday that will be us again.*"

Was Rosine changing the subject?

"Why weren't you in school?" Cal asked.

"In Burundi, Mali and I couldn't go to public school because we were refugees and didn't have the correct documents." She shook her head. "The only school we could attend was a private school that my parents had to pay for."

"Did you ever go?"

"Yes. Sometimes my dad would get a job, and I could go for a time. I loved it. I loved my uniform and my friends. I loved learning. But then the money would run out. One time, the headmaster came into my classroom, grabbed me by the arm, and yanked me out in front of everyone. They used us as an example to the others—no money, no school."

"That's terrible," Cal said. But the story gave her a funny feeling too, because she was happy to miss school. She had loved doing virtual school during the pandemic. It was perfect. She could still see her teacher, without having to hear about the birthday parties or sleepovers she hadn't been invited to.

"I hate school," Cal blurted.

"Why?"

"I don't fit in there." Cal shrugged. "I feel less alone on the mountain with Wildcat than I do at school."

"I'm sorry you don't like it, but I'm there now."

Cal wondered if that was true. Part of her didn't want

to think past the mountain. Would Rosine still want to be friends if they found the magic? Or if they didn't?

"The sun's going to be up soon." Cal stood. "We need to get ready to climb."

Rosine tossed her backpack over her shoulder.

"Why do you carry that everywhere you go?" Cal asked.

"I'm used to carrying everything I own with me, I guess."

"Rosine . . . ," Cal began. She didn't like this feeling of distrust. She wanted her friend to know it was okay to tell her if she'd taken the box. If anyone knew about taking stuff that didn't belong to them, it was Cal.

But Rosine walked away. "I'll see what we have for water," she said before heading into the woods.

At the firepit, Cal found her boots where Rosine had left them. She dumped the rocks out and felt inside. They were warm and dry.

She inventoried what was left of their food. The bread and granola bars and beans were gone. There were only two cans of sardines left.

When Rosine came back, Cal held up a yellow tin. "This is all we have for breakfast," she said.

"But that's for Wildcat." Rosine looked around. "Where is he?"

"I didn't see him when I got up. He's probably hunting somewhere." She wondered how mad he'd be if they shared his breakfast. She peeled open a yellow tin and sniffed. *"Blech!* I can't eat this." She placed it on a rock and called, "Wildcat!"

But the only response was the shriek of a hawk circling above.

"He'll find it when he's hungry."

Each girl put on her climbing shoes and stepped into a harness. Cal helped Rosine tighten the waist belt and double back the buckles.

"Where is that tool that Ms. Adelman used?" Rosine asked. "The one that holds the rope so we don't fall."

"You mean the belay device." Cal handed Rosine a black metal object. "This is called an ATC. There's no top rope coming down from the peak, so we're going to multi-pitch trad climb."

"What does that mean?"

"We'll take turns belaying each other as we climb. The spire is about one hundred feet. Like I explained before, I'll insert protection along the way so that if we slip, the stoppers will arrest any falls. We'll do the climb in four pitches, which is more than we need to, but it will be safer that way. First, you'll belay me while I climb. When I reach the top of the first pitch, I'll insert three stoppers and clip my harness to them with an equalized corde-lette so I'm anchored. Then I'll belay you from where I am above you. When you reach me, you'll clip into the anchor and I'll move on to the next pitch and anchor in again. We'll keep doing that until we're at the top."

"Got it," Rosine said.

"Okay, let's tie up." Cal chose the green thirty-meter rope. Do you remember how to make the knots?" She handed one end to Rosine.

"I think so."

"Watch me," Cal said, letting her end of the rope touch the ground. She bent it where it met her waist. "Here's our guy." She picked up the end. "Give him a tie."

"Then poke him in the eye." Rosine giggled.

Cal nodded, immediately feeling better. Rosine's cour-age was making her feel braver again. *I got this*, she thought. After all, climbing was something she'd done her whole life.

"Now put the end through both tie-in points on your harness and do it again," Cal said.

"Two, four, six, eight, ten." Cal counted the ropes that made up the double figure eight. "All set." She took a deep breath. "Okay, now I'm going to attach the belay device." She made a bight in the rope and used a locking carabiner to attach it to Rosine's harness. "You need to hold on to the brake rope high with both hands, like this. As I climb, you keep giving me slack and work with me while I put in the stoppers every so often. If I fall, pull down on the brake strand like this, got it?"

"Yes, Ms. Adelman gave me extra lessons during study hall. I'm ready."

Both girls looked up. The spire's peak was obscured by a layer of clouds. "Are you sure you're ready for this?"

Rosine nodded. "One hundred percent."

Mr. Lopez's words seemed to fill Cal's head. *You're a good climber, Scott, but the spire?*

Cal stared hard at the mountain. "On belay?" she said to Rosine.

"Belay on," Rosine responded.

Cal leapt upward, tackling the mountain as if she were King Kong scaling the Empire State Building. She knew climbing was as much a mental game as a physical one. Right then she felt as if she'd been preparing for this her whole life. The cracks and ridges she clung to were narrow, but she had small hands and feet. Maybe that was why no one else had reached the peak. Maybe the spire was waiting for a kid.

She kept going, inserting protection along the way. When she was about a quarter of the way up, she inserted three stoppers. She used her cordelette to build an anchor, then attached her harness to it with two cara-biners. Her left arm was beginning to ache. She shook it out. "This is the first pitch," she called to Rosine. "I'm anchored in. I'm going to pull the rope up and put you on belay. Follow my path. It's not bad at all! Ready when you are!"

"Belay on?" Rosine called up.

"On belay," Cal responded.

Rosine reached for a handhold. At first, she seemed cautious, then quickly fell into a groove, gracefully scaling the spire. When she reached Cal, she was grinning. "That was better than I thought," she said.

Cal showed Rosine how to clip into the anchor. They managed the rope and began the same process for the second pitch. Cal started climbing.

Like the first pitch, she settled into a routine, moving quickly up the spire. After she'd covered about twenty feet, the hand- and footholds seemed to stretch farther apart. Her left arm began to throb like a toothache. She reached for a knob but didn't make it. She slipped, before jamming two fingers into a pocket in the rock.

"Are you okay?" Rosine shouted.

Cal clung to the spire. She was starting to lose her nerve.

"Are you at the second pitch?" Rosine called.

"Close enough." Cal shoved three stoppers into a crack and anchored in. In no time, Rosine was beside her.

"Do you want to rest? I can keep going," Rosine said.

"No." Cal shook out a spasm in her arm. "I have to insert the protection." They switched positions, and Cal took off again.

Grab. Step.

Her left arm was not working as it should.

Grab. Step.

Grab. Step.

She slipped before digging her foot into a crack. As she grabbed a jutting rock, her left shin scraped the mountain, and she felt the warm ooze of blood run down her leg.

"Are you okay?" Rosine called from below.

Mist had rolled in around Cal. She could hear Rosine, but she couldn't see her.

"I'm okay," Cal said, trying to assure herself too.

Grab. Step.

A million dots of vapor seemed to seep into her skin and enter her lungs. Dew collected on her face.

Breathe!

Grab. Step. Grab. Step.

She paused, jamming in three stoppers. "Off belay!" she called. After managing the rope, Cal said, "On belay. Come on up!"

Soon Cal could make out Rosine scrambling toward her as if she were Spider-Woman. She appeared so light and free. *I'm the one who's done this before.* As much as she wanted to ignore it, a new ember flickered. One of jealousy.

Rosine suddenly materialized in front of her.

"Third pitch," Cal said. "You made it." She was still catching her breath.

"Do you want me to keep going? The peak is right there," Rosine said, pointing upward.

Cal nodded. She clipped back in and belayed Rosine, who quickly disappeared inside the fog.

Then Cal did what a climber should never do. She looked down.

Her head spun as she clung to the mountain. She could barely make out the round stones of their firepit and the stick frame of their shelter.

Look up! She heard a voice inside her head. *Don't look down, look up!* It was like she was back with her dad on Ragged Mountain again.

Cal pulled herself away from the view, instead following the rope as it traveled up the spire and disappeared inside a cloud.

"Come on, Cal!" Rosine shouted. "There's a giant boulder here. I wrapped the rope around it. I got you!"

Cal reached for a knob. *Breathe. You know what to do.*

Step right foot high. There, up to your left, a piece of granite as tiny as a light switch. Reach. Grab. Pull. Step. Higher. Harder. No, not that hard. Focus. Breathe. Reach. Grab. Pull. Step.

It was coming back. She was in the zone—unable to tell where the mountain ended and she began.

And then she froze. The stone had turned smooth as a mirror. There was nothing left to hold. Not even the skinniest razor's edge to grip on to.

Cal squinted at the peak again, but it was still hiding inside a cloud.

"Rosine!" she shouted. "Where do I go?"

No answer.

What was I thinking? I can't do this, Cal thought.

Then Rosine's voice. "There's a rock that juts out. It's on the right . . . kind of far. You have to stretch."

From the corner of her eye, Cal saw what Rosine was talking about. She extended her foot, feeling for the knob. Her muscles began to shake.

"I can't reach it!"

"Yes, you can! Stretch!"

"I can't! I'm too tired and my arm isn't working right."

"I got you! You can do it."

Cal felt a firm tug on her waist.

Without notice, a gust of wind blew. The clouds parted, and she could see Rosine standing on the peak. She had tied the rope around the boulder and threaded it through her belay device. She gripped the rope in both hands.

"I'm telling you, I got you!" Rosine shouted.

With all her might, Cal extended her foot until she was almost doing a split. When she was about to give up, she felt the knob with the very tip of her toe. She shifted, then half leapt, hoping the foothold was where she thought it was. At the same time, she saw a pocket, barely wide enough for two fingers, above it. She reached as she planted her foot on the granite knob.

"Yes!" Rosine shouted.

As Rosine gathered slack, the rope between them tightened. It was as if Rosine's strength was traveling its length like electricity. Straight into Cal. Slowly, she began to climb again.

At that moment, her left hand slipped. It was enough to throw her off-balance. For a moment, she dangled loose of everything. She screamed as the harness cinched tight.

"Trust me!" Rosine screamed.

Cal knew that Rosine wouldn't let anything bad happen. She floated. The sky was above her. The earth below. And Rosine. Everything connected.

Right then, Cal spotted another knob and swung her foot toward it.

She was back on the mountain. *I got this. I got this.*

Now, she was only about fifteen feet from the top, but the wall still seemed too smooth to climb. *How in the world had Rosine done it?*

Just as she was about to give up, an errant ray of light hit the wall, illuminating a series of tiny cracks and fissures that traveled to its peak. It was as if the spire had laid out a ladder for her.

Cal dug her fingertips into each tiny crack, slowly crawling up. When she reached the top, she extended her arm. Rosine gripped her wrist.

As Cal looked up, she saw her hand fastened to Rosine's—threaded together in the most perfect knot . . .

Stronger than any rope.

She felt her body rise. With all her might, she crawled onto the spire and collapsed. She hugged the mountain.

Rosine leaned over her.

"We did it, Cal. We did it."

Chapter 18

Cal rolled onto her knees, using the white boulder to pull herself up. Her legs tingled, and she felt unsteady on her feet. A dull buzzing filled her head. Electricity coursed through her veins. She blinked hard, trying to force her eyes into focus.

Did we die? she wondered. *Is this heaven?*

As she slowly regained her senses, she realized that her foggy vision was caused by tiny drops of dew that floated all around her like soda bubbles. She licked her dry lips. They even tasted sweet.

"We did it," Cal said. "I can't believe it."

They were standing on top of the spire! Despite the

fog, Cal could see that the summit was larger and flatter than it appeared from the ground.

Rosine unwrapped the rope from around the boulder. "I'm going to explore," she said before disappearing inside the fog.

"Rosine!" Cal shouted after her. She couldn't see where she'd gone, but the rope was still attached to their harnesses, and Cal could feel it shift and tighten as Rosine moved about.

Cal touched her hand to her waist. "Rosine!" she shouted again. "Where are you?"

The tension on the rope went slack, and Rosine appeared again. Droplets of precipitation encircled her head as if she were wearing a sparkling crown.

"Isn't this the most beautiful place you've ever seen? It's perfect!" Rosine twirled as much as she could without becoming tangled in the rope.

"Perfect for what?" Cal asked.

Without answering, Rosine ran off. "Come on!" she said, again disappearing into the mist.

This time when Cal felt a tug, she followed. Up above the clouds, the world was silent except for the crunch of gravel beneath their feet.

At the edge of the spire, Cal looked down. The clouds

shifted, and there was Bleakerville, still looking like an old-fashioned postcard. There was the row of houses on Mountain Road, as small as Monopoly pieces. Beyond them, the steeple of the Congregational church, the dome of the synagogue, Bleaker K–8's dull brick rectangle, and the vacant glass factory.

But from this vantage, Cal could see much farther. The world beyond Bleakerville appeared wide and open. Across the horizon, larger mountains sprawled and reached, blue and bold against the gray sky. She quickly spotted Ragged Mountain. Even though it had a higher elevation than Mount Meteorite, from where she stood, it seemed to bow in respect.

Cal was on top of the world. She spun slowly. The sheer height of where she stood gave her some kind of superpower.

A breeze fluttered her hair and caressed her cheek. She closed her eyes, listening to the mountain breathe in and out, *You are home, you are home, you are home.*

"Isn't it magical?" Rosine asked.

Cal opened her eyes. For a moment she'd forgotten about their mission.

Magic.

She turned and scanned the peak as if looking for an arrow that read MAGIC METEORITE, THIS WAY!

But as she squinted and spun and searched, one thing became clear.

"There's nothing here," she said.

"What do you mean?" Rosine held her arms out wide. "There's everything here."

"Do you see a meteorite?"

"Isn't it that big white boulder I wrapped the rope around?"

Cal walked back toward the boulder, pulling Rosine along with her.

"This is milky quartz," Cal said, examining it. "Meteorites are never made of quartz."

Rosine bent down, scooping up some of the sandy dirt that was scattered across the peak. "Maybe this *is* the meteorite—maybe it exploded?"

Cal watched the gravel sift through Rosine's fingers.

"Are you kidding? That's dirt."

And then Cal did what she always did when she became sad or disappointed or worried or scared. Cal got mad.

The ember of anger ignited so quickly she didn't have time to even think about extinguishing it.

"There's nothing here but that white boulder and all this . . . dirt." Cal drew her foot back and kicked the boulder as if it were responsible for the barren peak. Pain shot up her leg.

"Stop it," Rosine said.

Cal threw her hands in the air. "You are a fraud!" she shouted at the spire. "A trick! Where is the magic? Huh?"

She took a few steps back, then ran toward the white boulder as if she were going to tackle it. She closed her eyes for impact. She wanted to hurt. She wanted her outsides to feel like her insides did. The same way they did on *the day when everything changed.*

But right as Cal was about to hit the boulder full force, her entire body jerked back.

"What the . . . ?" she shouted.

She turned to see Rosine gripping the rope. She had stopped the impact.

Tears sprang to Cal's eyes. "Why did you do that?"

Every wound on Cal's body began to ache. Her bloodied shin, her weak arm, her leg where she'd kicked the spire. Her heart.

Rosine moved next to her. "I'm not going to let you hurt yourself."

Cal turned away. "Everything we did was for nothing. The planning, gathering the equipment . . ." She tugged at her harness. "The exploring I did, the maps I made, the gear I found, leaving at dawn, lying to my mom . . ." She wanted to kick the boulder again, but Rosine gripped the rope firmly. "All because I fell for a make-believe fairy tale told to kids."

"But we never knew what the meteorite was supposed to look like." Rosine reached down, grabbing another handful of the sandy dirt. "How do you know this isn't the magic?"

Cal considered what Rosine said. The truth was she didn't know what the meteorite looked like. No one did. But the way she felt each time she watched the peak erupt in flame made her certain that the magic they were looking for had to be more than the gray rubble before them.

"It was supposed to look like fire on ice," Cal shouted as she scooped up her own fistful of dirt. "Not this!" She threw it as hard as she could. Gravel sprayed everywhere. She picked up another and threw it too.

"Stop," Rosine said. "Please?"

But Cal kept throwing dirt. She knew it was something a five-year-old would do, but she didn't care. Somehow, she found power in her anger.

"It was a lie!" Cal shouted. "There is no magic!" Soon tears streamed down her face. "There's only awful and bad and wrong." She sat down hard and covered her face with her hands. "I can't believe I fell for that story. I can't believe we came here for nothing."

"I don't think it was for nothing."

"Well, you can think whatever you want." Cal turned to her. "Why aren't you mad? Don't you understand, Rosine? We lost. Your sister . . . she's going to stay sad. And you're going to have to move to the city, and my mom—" She couldn't say it. She couldn't admit what it meant not to find the meteorite. Cal crumbled as if her bones had melted. "What if she dies?"

Rosine put a hand on her shoulder. "I know this is hard, Cal. But I also know that *you* will be okay. I know this because you are strong."

Cal shook her off angrily. "Are you listening?" she screamed. "I'm talking about my mother. My mother is going to die. That's why I'm here. But now . . ." She leapt up, kicking the milky-quartz boulder again before Rosine could stop her. Pain shot up her leg. "There is no magic! Don't you get it? I didn't save my mother!"

"Look at me," Rosine said calmly.

Cal ignored her, but Rosine moved in front of her, forcing their eyes to meet.

"My mother," Rosine began. "She died."

Tears filled Cal's eyes. "I know, Rosine, you told me. I'm sor—"

"Listen," Rosine interrupted. "I'm trying to tell you

that no matter how many days and nights I cried and prayed and begged, she died anyway."

Cal's eyes grew large.

Rosine held her gaze. "But I survived, Cal. I survived that, and a war and prejudice and a flight across the world to this strange place where I didn't even understand one word."

Cal blinked. Of course she knew that. She'd heard Rosine tell her stories, but at the same time, it hadn't sunk in. Not really. Before that moment, the people Rosine talked about were like paper dolls. It wasn't until that very second, looking directly into her deep brown eyes, the realization washed over her. Rosine's mother—her *mom*—had died.

And Rosine kept living.

Cal's bottom lip began to quiver. She bit it as the ember erupted all over again.

"No! You're not supposed to say that to me!" she shouted. "You're supposed to say, *Don't worry, Cal, she'll be fine!* That's what you're supposed to say!" The anger flamed hot. "Just because your mother died doesn't mean mine will." As the words came out of her mouth, she knew how mean and awful they sounded, but Cal was feeling mean and awful inside.

Rosine blinked.

"You're supposed to say . . ." Cal took a breath and began again. "What you are supposed to say is, *Don't worry, Cal, your mom will be fine. Don't worry, Cal, your mom is soooo strong. She'll get through this.* For your information, that is what a *friend* tells another *friend*!"

Rosine's face was a blank slate. "But that's not always the truth," she said. "Sometimes there isn't enough magic in the world to change that. Do you think your mother has more right to live than mine?"

Cal felt as though she'd been gut-punched. And then the heavy weight was back on her chest. The rock that seemed to press everything out of her—air, sadness, hope—all at once.

"Magic or no magic, there are things we can't control," Rosine said.

"Then why are you here, Rosine? If you don't believe in the magic, why did you climb the spire?"

"I have my reasons." Rosine stared into the horizon. "And I never said I didn't believe."

The hollow-tree feeling washed through Cal. She scanned the gray and gravelly landscape. "How did I think this was beautiful?" She kicked at the dirt. "It's ugly."

As if on cue, dark clouds scudded across the peak. The sky turned black. For a millisecond, Cal had one of those déjà vu moments. She had been with her father on Mount Washington. *There's a storm coming. We need to go now.*

"We need to go," Cal said. "Now."

Standing on either side of the boulder, they stared down the path they'd climbed up. Their campsite appeared distant and small.

Cal bit her lip. Hard. She'd spent so much time worrying about how to get up the spire, she hadn't thought about getting down. She knew that's when most accidents happened.

"We're going to have to down-climb," Cal said.

"What does that mean?"

"Climb backward the way we came." Cal tucked a loose strand of hair behind her ear. "But it's really hard, because you can't see where you're going." She thought for a minute, putting her hand on the milky-quartz boulder. "Or . . . maybe we can rappel using this."

"What's *rappel*?" Rosine asked.

"I'll show you. We'll need the longer rope." She dug inside her backpack and pulled out the red rope. "Good," she said. "Rappel means to lower yourself down from a high place. We'll walk backward down the rock face, like you did in gym class, but we'll each use our own ATC belay devices to control how fast we go. I've never done it myself, but I've seen my dad do it."

197

Cal wrapped the center of the red rope around the white boulder. She made stopper knots at the end of each rope before draping them over the side of the spire. They dangled several feet from the ground. "Now hand me your ATC," she said when she was finished.

"Hold on." Rosine suddenly ran off, again disappearing in the fog.

"What are you doing?" Cal shouted.

But the thick air swallowed her words.

"Rosine!" Cal called again.

And then she was back.

"Where did you go?"

"The dirt," Rosine said, patting the pocket on her hoodie. "Remember, I collect dirt."

"You had to do that right now?" Cal rolled her eyes. "I need your belay device."

Rosine handed it to her, and Cal grabbed hold of one of the ropes. Bending it, she inserted the bight into the device, then attached it to Rosine's harness with a locking carabiner. Then she did it again with the other rope and her own belay device. She tested it.

"I did it," Cal said. "I can't believe it."

"Of course you did," Rosine said.

Cal tugged at the rope. "The belay creates tension.

We have to feed our rope through the devices at the same speed. Since I'm on one end of the rope, and you're on the other, we'll offset each other. I keep you from falling, and you keep me from falling."

A flash of lightning lit the sky.

"One last thing is I'm going to attach this sling to both of our harnesses. It will help us stay together." The damp air made her hands sticky, and every now and then she wiped her palms on her jeans.

When she finished, they took their places on either side of the white boulder. "Ready?" Cal asked.

"I'm glad we can't see where we're going," Rosine said.

"Keep looking forward. I'm going to count. On *three*, we'll both start walking backward," Cal said.

Rosine nodded.

"Ready?"

"Yes."

"One, two, three." The girls began their descent.

Another flash filled the sky, followed by a loud *boom!*

Cal's shoulders jerked.

"It's okay," she said. "Steady and even. This storm is coming fast."

A gust of wind rushed at the peak; for a second Cal felt off-balance.

"Hold on!" she shouted.

The wind swept away the fog, revealing a crisp, clear world.

Cal blinked.

Crack! Lightning flashed.

As it did, Cal saw something sitting in the middle of the spire that hadn't been there a moment ago.

She squinted at the object. Her vision fogged and cleared . . . fogged and cleared, until she could make out what it was.

The box.

The half-moon-shaped carved wooden box she'd found in the cave with the word.

"Wait! Stop!" Cal shouted. "We need to go back!" She had to make sure it was the same box she'd seen in the cave. If it was, then it definitely had something to do with the meteorite. That word—*amani*—it had to be a clue.

Even though Rosine was next to her, she acted as if she couldn't hear Cal. She kept moving downward as if caught in a trance.

Cal had no choice but to keep up. If she didn't, they'd both fall. As they kept their steady pace, a million questions swirled inside Cal's head. And one answer—Rosine.

Soon they reached the start of the third pitch.

"Rosine!" Cal shouted over the growing wind. "You had that box all along!"

But Rosine still didn't respond.

When they reached the second pitch, Cal tried again. "Why did you leave it there? It was a clue!"

Rosine sped up, forcing Cal to as well.

By the time they reached the last pitch, large wet drops had begun to fall. At first, Cal welcomed the rain. She lifted her face to the sky and opened her mouth, letting it soothe her parched mouth. As she did, her foot slipped, and she had no choice but to reach for the mountain. Her hand found a knob, and she held on for dear life.

"Are you okay?" Rosine called.

Now it was Cal's turn not to answer. She pressed her cheek into the granite, feeling its roughness. She couldn't take one more thing going wrong.

"Why are you doing this to me?" She wasn't sure if she was asking the mountain or Rosine.

"We need to go, Cal," Rosine said.

But Cal didn't budge.

"We need to get out of here."

The wind gusted.

"You can't be mad at me, Cal."

Cal ignored her, instead looking down at their

campsite below. The wind had blown away the leaves, making their shelter look like a large animal skeleton.

"I—I can't do it, Rosine."

"What? Yes, you can. Come on, Cal. Let's go."

Cal shook her head.

"What about Wildcat?" Rosine blurted. "You have to keep going so you can find Wildcat. Don't you want to make sure he ate his breakfast?"

"Wildcat?"

"Yeah. Come on. We need to find him before the storm gets worse. He's probably looking for you," Rosine said.

Something clicked inside Cal. "Wildcat," she said. "I need to find Wildcat." She lifted her body away from the mountain. When she was in position, the two began walking backward again until they were a few feet from the ground.

Then Cal jumped.

Chapter 19

As she hit the landing, Cal tugged off her harness and ran to the firepit, where she'd left the sardines.

The food was untouched.

Cal spun, frantically searching. The skies had opened, drenching her hair and clothes. She stared at the shelter. Only half the sticks and branches were left.

"We can't stay here!" Rosine shouted over the growing wind. She grabbed Cal's arm and pulled.

"Don't touch me!" Cal yelped as if in pain.

Rosine yanked her hand back.

"I have to find Wildcat!" Cal said.

The wind was blowing so hard now she had to fight

against it to stay standing. "Wildcat!" she called over its whine. "Wildcat! Where are you?"

There was a crack of thunder.

"Cal!" Rosine shouted. "Wildcat will be okay. Remember what you told me? Wildcat finds you. Always!"

"But what if he doesn't? What if he's lost?" Cal felt the wind pull her sideways.

"If we don't get out of here, this wind is going to blow us over the edge. I'll bet Wildcat is in the forest. Come on!"

Cal scanned Jacob's Landing once more before following Rosine into the woods. Soon, they came to the bean cans that they'd left to collect water. Cal was reaching for one when an enormous cracking noise filled the air. *Whoosh!* A tree fell behind her, its roots screaming as they ripped from the earth.

This time when Rosine grabbed Cal's hand, she let her take it.

She closed her eyes against the blinding rain, holding tight to Rosine as they ran. When they stopped, Cal could see that they were standing in front of the giant fallen ash tree.

Rosine pointed to its massive underground dirt cave. "We need to go in there."

"What if there's already someone living in it? Like a bear!"

A crack of lightning, followed by a thunderous *BOOM!* Cal felt as shocked as if she'd been struck.

"We don't have time to find out!" Rosine pushed aside the dangling curtain of roots and pulled Cal in behind her. A shower of dirt fell in Cal's hair, but as soon as they were tucked inside, the loud whine of wind softened. Cal breathed the familiar smells of damp earth and bark. Rain fell in sheets outside. Her heartbeat slowed.

She scooted away from Rosine, squatting directly behind the curtain of roots.

Cal removed her backpack and dug inside it for a flashlight. She flicked it on, but it didn't work. When her eyes adjusted to the underground darkness, she could see that the root-cave was empty, as if the tree had saved this place just for them. They were safe. But still . . .

"Wildcat," Cal moaned.

She leaned forward, peering through the long, stringy root curtain. Rain washed by like a river's current.

She cupped her hands around her mouth. Leaning into the root-curtain entrance, she shouted, "WILD-CAT! PLEASE COME!" She dug inside her backpack and pulled out the last yellow tin. She peeled it open. The smell of fish filled the damp cave. She placed it at the entrance.

"WILDCAT! I HAVE SARDINES!" she yelled through

the root curtain. Tears sprang to her eyes, but she continued to call over and over and over until her voice gave way to a raspy cough.

Rosine placed a warm hand on her trembling shoulder. "It will be okay," she said. "Everything will be okay."

Cal spun on her. "How many times do I have to tell you not to *touch* me!" she shouted.

Rosine scooted back so quickly she fell over. Mud seeped into her pants.

"You keep saying everything will be okay, *You'll be fine, Cal*," she said, mimicking Rosine. "But you don't know what you're talking about."

Rosine's eyes grew large.

"For the record"—Cal's voice trembled—"I'm sick of your stories. And you know what else, Rosine? I think you're a liar!"

"You can believe or not believe. That is your problem, not mine," Rosine said. "But I know what's real and what isn't. What you are saying—that's your truth, not mine."

"What are you talking about?" Cal was so angry she spit the words out.

"You are angry because you think your mother is leaving you on purpose. You're mad at her for being sick."

Boom! The clap of thunder was so powerful Cal felt it reverberate throughout her hollow body.

"What? How dare you!" Cal grabbed a clump of cold, wet earth as if she were going to throw it at Rosine. Instead, she closed her fist on it, letting the mud ooze through her fingers.

"I know you took the wooden box that was in the cave. I saw it on the spire." She glared at Rosine. "You lied to me! You said you went back to take dirt, but you were really hiding it there so you can go back and find the magic meteorite by yourself. You are a liar! And a thief too."

"I am none of those things!"

Cal grabbed the purple backpack. "What else did you steal when I wasn't looking?"

"I have taken nothing of yours," Rosine said.

Cal opened the backpack and shook it out, but the bag was empty. "Well, there's nothing in here now, but I know you were hiding the wooden box all along!" She threw the bag on the ground. "Answer me! Why did you take it?"

That's when Cal heard the sniffling.

Rosine was crying.

Cal had never seen her cry.

She'd never seen her get angry or scared or tired or defeated.

Cal sucked in her breath, feeling her own anger

dissolve, as if Rosine's tears were the one thing that could reach her heart.

She immediately wanted to swallow back her hate-filled words, but they seemed to be floating around the dirt cave, out of reach.

"Rosine." Cal cleared her throat. Her voice was hoarse and weak. "I—I'm sorry—I don't know why I . . . I didn't mean any of that."

Silence.

Each word cut like a razor in her throat, but Cal forced them out anyway. "Rosine . . . I'm . . . so—"

"Shut up, Cal, okay? Just . . . stop talking." Rosine wiped her face with her sleeve, then crawled to the farthest corner of the shelter.

Cal turned away. She adjusted her body so she could gaze through the tree-root curtain at the can of sardines she'd left outside.

It spilled with rainwater.

She glanced back to the corner Rosine had holed herself up in, but it was dark and silent.

Tears poked from the corners of Cal's eyes. She tried to hold them back, but it was useless. Soon she resembled the world outside as tears streamed down her face, thick and powerful as the steady rain.

Chapter 20

It was the silence that woke Cal.

She'd fallen asleep behind the tree-root curtain, waiting for Wildcat to come. Or Rosine to leave. What time had that been? Two P.M.? Three P.M.? She didn't mean to fall asleep, but she was exhausted, inside and out.

Now it was night. The world was dark and quiet. The storm had ended.

She crawled outside. The air was so cold she could see her breath. A full moon illuminated the star-filled sky.

At some point before she fell asleep, she'd removed her climbing shoes. Now, cold wet dirt and rotting leaves squeezed between her toes.

She stumbled through the woods in a daze. The night

was so dense she felt as invisible as a ghost drifting about a spooky world.

Exiting the forest, she made her way across Jacob's Landing, feeling its smooth, cold granite below her feet. Soon she found herself standing on its fingertip-ledge. Her toes gripped its rough edges. She inhaled deeply as if trying to fill herself with the clear, cool night.

Without her heavy backpack, a lightness swept over her. Her arms floated out and up as if someone were lifting them. The thick black night washed around her like a river current, levitating her body as if in a magician's trick.

"This is what it feels like to fly," she said to no one. She went up on her toes as if her whole body might spontaneously rise off the ground. As she did, a small piece of ledge below gave way. She flapped her arms against the sudden shift in gravity, but that just caused her to lose control. She fell fast.

Down, down, down. Her arms flailed as she tried to reach for the mountain, but she was moving too fast. Jagged rock slashed her fingertips like razors. She jerked her hand back, but as she did, she felt a pronounced *thwack* as her left elbow banged against rock. She immediately cradled the bruise as she fell deeper into the night.

But instead of panic, a strange sensation came over her. Suddenly, nothing hurt. Not the left elbow of her newly uncasted arm or the bump on her head. Not the blisters on her heels or her bruised and bleeding shin.

Pebbles and gravel fell around her like shooting stars.

So beautiful, she thought. She reached out to touch one, but as she did, she stopped falling because at that moment, someone grabbed her hand.

Cal's feet dangled.

She lifted her chin so that she faced the mountain. Then she looked up.

"Mr. Demsky?" she said. "What are you doing here?"

With a giant tug, Cal was whooshed back to where she'd been standing.

"Why don't we move back a few steps, hey?" Mr. Demsky chuckled as he guided her backward.

Cal glanced sideways at the man. He was dressed for work in his old blue flannel shirt with the hole in the elbow and his baggy pants. A long white apron was tied around his waist.

He leaned down to pick up his cane before tugging on his left suspender strap. Even though she couldn't see his mouth beneath his bushy white mustache, somehow she knew he was smiling.

His face turned serious. "So, did you find it?"

Cal blinked. None of this made sense.

Find? Find something?

Mr. Demsky laughed a booming laugh that was so loud and deep it echoed across the mountain like thunder.

"The magic, of course!"

"No." Cal frowned. "You know I didn't."

"Really?"

"You knew there was no magic meteorite. It was a made-up story for kids, like my mom said. And Mr. Lopez. A fiction. A fantasy."

Thunder-laughter came again, loud and booming and rumbling so deep Cal felt it vibrate through her bones.

"I don't know what's so funny," she said. "Do you enjoy tricking kids and making them climb dangerous mountains and almost die?"

"I've seen you climb, Cal. I knew you could scale the spire. I wasn't tricking anyone."

Cal wanted to kick something. The dirt, a large rock, Mr. Demsky. She felt her hands form fists.

"I was up there. I saw the peak. There's nothing there!" she screamed.

"Some people only see me as a store clerk, Cal, but you know, I'm a scientist too."

Cal crossed her arms. It was just like Mr. Demsky to talk nonsense when she wanted facts.

"And?" She knew how rude she sounded, but she

didn't care. She stared hard at the old man, noticing for the first time that his eyes were sparkling as bright as stars.

"If you believe you're looking at a rock, Cal . . . well, then that's what you'll see."

"I'm sick of your riddles," she said angrily. "You say you're a scientist, but you're not. Well, I am! From now on, I want facts. I'm done with fairy tales. And I'm done with magic!"

"Remember when you were in the back office with Rosine? You asked me a question. What was it?"

"What? I don't know."

"Yes, you do."

Why did it feel like Mr. Demsky was always inside her head?

She closed her eyes. "You said something like, *when you believe . . . that's when the impossible becomes possible, and you'll find the magic.*" She took a breath, then opened her eyes. "And I said, *what am I supposed to believe in?*"

"That's right."

"And you never answered me."

"Right again," he said. His eyes glittered like polished gemstones.

"So?" Cal asked impatiently.

"Think about it, Cal. Maybe you'll see that you found the magic after all."

As Cal studied the old man, she felt drawn into his star-eyes.

Mr. Demsky grinned broadly. Even his teeth seemed to sparkle. "I have to go now, Cal," he said.

"Go? Already? I thought you came to find us . . . to rescue us."

"Oh, come now. You know that you don't need me or anyone else to rescue you. Isn't that what you came here to do?"

Again with the riddles.

"I thought maybe my mom had sent you. That she was worried about me."

"Your parents *are* worried. You need to go home right away."

Cal exhaled, unsure why her mother being worried made her feel better.

"But I never found the magic."

"Haven't you?"

"No!" Cal screamed. "I don't know why I listened to you! It's not like you showed us any proof. It was all fake!"

"I know exactly what is on top of the spire."

"How?"

Before Mr. Demsky could answer, a noise interrupted them.

The sound of chattering teeth.

"Cal?"

She turned to face Rosine.

"Who are you talking to?" Rosine asked.

"Rosine! Tell Mr. Demsky there was nothing but quartz and dirt on the peak. Tell him—" Cal turned back. "Hey! Where did he go?"

Rosine rubbed her eyes. "Where did who go? There's no one here, Cal."

"He . . . Mr. Demsky . . . he was right here. I was standing out there . . ." Cal pointed to the edge. "I slipped and fell and . . ." She stared at Rosine. "What are you doing here?"

Rosine hugged herself. "I woke up and you weren't there. I was worried."

Before Cal could respond, Rosine walked to the edge. "You fell? Down there?" They both peered into the darkness. "If you fell down there, you'd still be there."

Cal kicked at a stone. The girls watched it plummet, bouncing off the jutting edges of the mountain. After a moment, they couldn't see it anymore, but they could still hear it. Chipping and breaking and falling.

"I did . . . I know I did." She touched the tender egg-sized lump on her elbow.

"Mr. Demsky?" Rosine yawned. "Yeah, I can picture him climbing up here with his cane." She laughed. "Come on, Cal. You were sleepwalking."

"But . . . it was so real." She followed Rosine to their dirt cave. As she stared at Rosine's back, she felt . . . something. Something she hadn't felt in a long time. She wanted to lean into her friend. She wanted to hug her and cry on her shoulder and thank her for coming to find her.

That is, until the events of the night before flashed through her brain.

A word lodged in Cal's throat, but when she tried to say it . . . it got caught.

Back inside the tree-root shelter, Rosine tucked herself into her corner. Cal squatted inside the root curtain and peered into the night.

When Cal was sure Rosine had fallen asleep, she turned to face her slumbering body.

"I'm sorry," she said.

And in the darkness of that damp, dirty place, Rosine whispered back.

"I know."

Chapter 21

"Cal. Cal, wake up!"

Cal's eyes fluttered open. For a moment she couldn't remember where she was. She groaned as she rolled away from the earth wall she'd been sleeping against. Her body screamed with pain. She blinked against the sunshine pouring through the tree-root curtain.

Rosine stood outside the entrance holding Cal's boots.

"Put these on and come on!" Rosine said before disappearing.

Cal crawled outside. She shoved her feet into the boots and made her way toward Rosine and the landing. Her stomach grumbled. She hugged her middle, trying to remember when they'd eaten last.

That was when she noticed Rosine squatting in front of what was left of their stick shelter.

What is she doing? she wondered.

As she got closer, she froze.

Half hidden beneath branches, dead leaves, and debris was Wildcat.

He lay motionless. Eyes closed. A pool of blood puddled beside his body.

"Wildcat!" Cal raced over, skidding to her knees.

He barely lifted his head before it fell again. Cal reached for him.

Rosine blocked her hand. "Don't touch him."

"What happened?"

"He must have been in a fight or was attacked."

Rosine gently removed the dried grass and leaves that covered the lower part of his body. Sticky red blood had dried in his fur.

Cal yelped as if feeling his pain.

"Wait here." Rosine leapt up, returning a moment later with her backpack. "We have to get him home right away. He needs a doctor," she said.

"But there are no animal hospitals in Bleakerville. We'll have to take him to the city and—"

"We don't have time for that. Mali will know what to do. She's always helped stray animals."

Cal looked hard at Rosine. She knew what it meant to leave now. To quit. No matter what Mr. Demsky had told her last night, if that was even real, Cal knew that leaving now meant she'd never find the magic. She also knew she didn't have a choice.

The girls carefully placed Wildcat inside Rosine's backpack. He didn't make a sound.

"Don't leave me, Wildcat. I—I need you." Cal took the backpack. "He's my responsibility. I'll carry him." She put it on in front, leaving the top of the bag open so she could keep an eye on him.

Rosine nodded.

As they headed into the forest, the reality of the situation flooded over Cal. *By now, Mom has to know I never made it to Aunt Viola's.*

Still, Cal was confused. Wouldn't her mother have thought to look on the mountain where Cal spent all her free time? And if so, where were the search parties? Where were the rangers and volunteers she'd seen on the TV news when hikers got lost on other mountains? Did her mother even care she was gone?

Sadness and disappointment only compounded the hollowness she already felt.

The girls made their way past the dirt cave. Cal fought to stay focused on her surroundings. She couldn't afford to get lost again. She literally had Wildcat's life in her hands. She felt as if she were wading through cement, but she pushed through it.

Finally, they came to the oak split down the middle like an uppercase *V*, and Cal breathed a sigh of relief. They were on the right track.

Downward they continued until they reached the bushwhacked trail that led to the well-worn path and the yellow sign that announced, WELCOME TO MOUNT METE-ORITE, BLEAKERVILLE'S HIDDEN MAGIC.

The closer to home they got, the heavier Cal's shoulders felt under the weight of Rosine's backpack. By the time they made it to the carriage house, the bag felt as if it weighed a million pounds.

In the post-storm, hazy sunshine, Cal realized how they appeared.

Rosine had mud on her face and Wildcat's blood on her shirt. Her jeans were dirty and ripped where she'd been nicked climbing the mountain.

Cal studied her own wounds. The cut on her shin had opened again, and fresh blood soaked her jeans. Her fingertips were sliced from climbing the spire, and the egg-shaped lump on her elbow had turned a mix of purple and green. When she ran a hand through her hair, she felt dirt and leaves and debris.

"Well, we're a pair," Rosine said.

Cal nodded.

"I guess I should take Wildcat now," Rosine said.

As Cal gently handed her the backpack, the front door of the carriage house flew open. A woman who looked like an older version of Rosine came flying out. She wore a yellow cotton dress and a matching scarf around her head.

"Rosine! Ulikuwa wapi?"

She tried to wrap her arms around Rosine, but Wildcat was in the way.

Mali stared hard at her sister. "Kwanini uko na uyo paka?"

A discussion ensued in which Cal couldn't quite tell if Mali was angry or relieved or both.

"Come on," Rosine finally said to Cal. "Mali knows what to do."

Inside the small home, there wasn't much furniture, but there was a warmth that seemed to blend perfectly with a delicious spicy scent. Cal hugged herself, unsure where to stand or what to do.

She looked around. The walls were empty except for a few pictures Cal was sure Mrs. Demsky had put up. Along the windowsill sat a row of five tiny jars. Although each held barely a tablespoon of dirt, Cal knew they represented so much more.

Rosine spread a blanket across a wooden table and Mali gently lifted Wildcat onto it. "Boil water," she said to Rosine, who immediately began to fill a pot.

"Hold him in place while I prepare!" Mali said to Cal.

Cal's eyes stung. Her lower lip began to tremble.

"We don't have time for tears," Mali said. "If you want to help, you need to be strong. Otherwise, go."

Cal blinked. She knew Mali wasn't being mean. She was being honest.

Cal sucked in her breath as she placed a hand on Wildcat, careful to avoid his wound. Wildcat made a gurgling sound.

"You're okay, my friend," Cal murmured. "You are strong and beautiful. You will get through this. Everything will be okay."

Rosine brought washcloths and a basin of steaming water. Mali wiped away blood. Wildcat made a guttural groaning noise.

"Is he going to die?" Cal whimpered.

"I don't know," Mali said. She turned to Rosine. "This animal's wound needs sewing. Bring me my kit."

"Stitches?" Cal said. "Won't that hurt him?"

Rosine ducked into the back room. Mali turned to Cal. "See, the wound. It is in a bad place. If it is not sewn, it will not heal."

As hard as Cal was trying not to cry, tears began to roll down her cheeks. She wiped them away with the back of her hand.

"I think you should go to your house now," Mali said. Her words seemed strict, but her voice was gentle.

"But—"

"It's better if there are only two of us working."

Cal tried to catch Rosine's eye, but she was busy gathering supplies.

At the door, Cal gave Wildcat one last glance, then she closed it behind her.

Outside, the little bit of sunshine she'd seen earlier had been swallowed by heavy gray clouds. Cal jammed her fists in her pockets as she looked down the street.

Debris from the storm littered Mountain Road. The remainder of leaves on the sycamore were gone. Its skeleton branches reached for an empty gray sky. The crooked shutter from her house now lay scattered in pieces across their front lawn.

Cal thought about heading back to the cave, but she knew she couldn't stand being there without Wildcat. Or Rosine.

Instead, she stumbled down the hill toward her own broken home.

Chapter 22

The closer Cal got to her house, the more she felt as though she were sleepwalking. At the Demskys', several cars filled the driveway and spilled into the road.

The couple always seemed to be hosting one meeting or another, so she wasn't surprised. She was disappointed, though. Life on Mountain Road seemed to have continued as usual without her.

She wanted to barge into their tidy cottage and confront Mr. Demsky. She wanted to ask if that really was him on Jacob's Landing. And if it wasn't, why did she have an egg-sized lump on her elbow?

None of it made sense.

And yet . . .

She'd hoped the old man would be on his porch, gazing at the spire as pipe smoke encircled his head. Talking mountains and magic. But no one was outside. Even the curtains had been drawn shut.

A car drove up and parked. Two elderly people dressed in black got out and walked up the steps onto the Demskys' front porch. They went inside, not seeming to notice the raggedy girl standing there.

Cal lowered her head and moved on.

While she made her way across brown grass, a million things spun in her head. What would Mom say? Would she be mad? Relieved? Or worse yet, what if she hadn't even noticed? What if she never realized Cal had been gone for two days and two nights?

But as Cal reached her home, she froze. Tucked in the driveway on the far side of the house was a police cruiser. Its black-and-white exterior stood out—clean and crisp against the dull green of the Scott home.

Cal's heart dropped as she slammed up the front steps and threw open the door.

"Mom!" she shouted. "Mom! Are you okay?"

"Cal!" a voice called.

A voice that wasn't Mom's.

Cal spun to see her father sitting in the family room with two uniformed police officers.

"Dad?"

Her father leapt up, racing to the door. "Oh, Cal, Cal . . . we were so worried."

She took a step back, staring at him as if he were a ghost. This seemed to make him freeze in place.

The officers closed their notepads.

"Calliope Scott?" The woman officer stood and walked toward her until they were face-to-face. "Are you okay? Do you need medical attention?"

Cal shook her head. "I'm fine." She turned away from the officer. "Dad, what are you doing here? Where's Mom?"

Her father ran a hand through his hair. "Cal . . . ," he began. "Mom . . ."

All the air went out of Cal's lungs.

The woman officer stared at Cal's torn jeans where the blood had dried. "What happened to you?" she asked.

"We were camping on the mountain. Me and my friend, Rosine. I scratched my leg on a rock." She showed the officer her leg. "But it's fine. Really. I'm okay. I just need to see my mom."

The officer turned toward Cal's father. "Looks like a flesh wound. You'll get her to a clinic if anything changes."

"Of course," he said.

The male officer joined his partner. "We'll let you two talk."

Cal's father nodded. "Thank you," he said to them. "Thank you for coming and thank you for . . . everything. We really appreciate your help." He began to follow them to the door, then paused at the kitchen table, gripping the back of a chair as if to steady himself.

"We're glad you're safe, Calliope," the officer said as he left.

Cal began to shake.

"Come here." Dad pulled out the chair he'd been leaning against. "Have a seat."

"No." Her entire body felt numb. "I want Mom. Where is she?"

"She's not here, Cal." Tears filled his eyes, and he took a deep breath. "On Saturday morning, Mrs. Demsky came over to tell Mom . . . well, some bad news." He sniffed, as if trying to figure out what to say. "When she got here, she found Mom with a very high fever." He cleared his throat. "Too high."

Cal wouldn't look at her father. Instead she turned, focusing her gaze on the fist-size hole in the wall.

Early Saturday morning was when Cal had stood in her mother's doorway, willing her to wake up.

"Mom apparently was incoherent. She kept repeating herself . . . saying your name . . . but she wasn't making sense because of the fever, I guess." He took a breath.

"Mrs. Demsky didn't know where you were . . . but then she discovered your note." He sighed. "Mom would have seen right through it . . . but she never had a chance to find it."

Cal covered her ears as if that could make everything go away. She didn't want to think about how she'd abandoned her mother when she'd needed her most. Or how Cal had lied.

"It's my fault . . . I made her sick. I thought I was helping . . . ," she began. "But I made everything worse."

"Mom is stable. She's at Memorial Hospital." Her father looked directly into Cal's eyes. "You didn't make her sick, Cal. The cancer did." He took a deep breath. "The good thing is that when she's stronger, the doctors have agreed to go forward with the surgery."

"I thought it was too dangerous."

"They have no choice. If they don't do it, she'll . . ." But her father didn't finish. He didn't need to.

Cal stumbled back. Her father immediately leapt up. "It's okay," he said, easing her into a chair. "The surgery's scheduled for later this week. We can see her tomorrow."

"I'm not going."

"Of course you're going. We can't stay long, but it's important to—"

"To what? To say goodbye?"

"No, Cal. To pray, to support, to have faith."

Cal shook her head. "How would we even get there? You can't take us." She knew it was a mean thing to say, but she was feeling mean. "And Mr. Demsky won't drive in the city."

"Oh, Cal. You don't know."

"Don't know what?"

Her father lowered his head. "Mr. Demsky . . . he died."

"What?"

"He's been ill for a while. He didn't want anyone to know." Dad sighed. "He died peacefully in his sleep."

"When?"

"Three days ago. That's what Mrs. Demsky was coming to tell Mom on Saturday morning."

"That's impossible."

"Cal . . ."

But Cal was already running.

Out the door, and past the old sycamore she'd hidden behind just a few nights ago while Mr. Demsky sat gazing at his mountain. Their mountain. Across the dried leaf lawn. She didn't care if she sounded like a herd of elephants as she pounded up the steps onto their crooked wooden porch. She threw open the door.

The Demskys' large front room was filled with people dressed in black. More black cloth draped over a mirror.

Mrs. Demsky and a young woman sat on low stools, while others stood or sat on chairs scattered around the room. A candle, set in the middle of a table, burned brightly.

There was a collective gasp as every head turned toward Cal. She looked down at her ripped jeans and remembered what she looked like.

Her first instinct was to bolt. To take off again running, as fast as possible.

But her feet had frozen in place.

Mrs. Demsky leaned forward, trying to stand from her low stool. The woman next to her helped her up. Cal immediately recognized her as Paloma—Mr. and Mrs. Demsky's daughter.

"Calliope Scott," Mrs. Demsky said. "Oh my goodness, what happened? Are you okay?"

Cal opened her mouth, but no words came out.

Paloma held her mother's hand as the two moved closer. Cal noticed they were each wearing a torn black ribbon.

"I—I'm okay. It's just a—" *A what?* she thought. *A skinned knee, a near-death experience, a dream . . . or maybe a nightmare?*

"Thanks to God you're all right, honey. We were so worried about you." Mrs. Demsky closed her eyes for a moment as if in prayer. Then she opened them again.

"Jacob. He always talked about you—you and his mountain," she said.

"Mr. Demsky talks about me?"

Dad was behind Cal now. He tugged on her sleeve. "We shouldn't be here right now."

"Simon," Mrs. Demsky said. "Come in. Have something to eat, please. It would mean so much to Jacob."

"Um, where is Mr. Demsky? I need to talk to—" Cal said.

Something about the way everyone began whispering made her bite her tongue.

"Why, Mr. Demsky has gone home, dear."

"Home?" Cal was getting frustrated. What were these people doing? Didn't they know she needed to talk to Mr. Demsky? Didn't they know it was important?

"What do you mean?" she said too loudly. "This *is* his home, and I need to talk to him. Now!"

"Cal!" Her father wasn't whispering anymore. He put a hand on her shoulder. She shook it off.

"No, honey, it's not." Mrs. Demsky sighed. "Mr. Demsky left this world on Friday."

Cal shook her head. "No! You're not listening to me." She could feel her voice rising, but she couldn't stop. "I saw him last night. I talked to him. He was on the mountain, and . . ." Her voice trailed off as guests shifted in their chairs. Someone got up and walked into the other room. Rain began to drum on the roof.

"Stop it, Cal. You're upsetting everyone," her father said. And then to the Demskys, "I'm so sorry. Cal's been . . ."

"Through a lot," Mrs. Demsky finished.

"But I did see him," Cal continued. "Last night! I fell, and he . . . he grabbed my hand." She showed Mrs. Demsky her elbow. "I got this bruise . . . and he was wearing his apron from the shop." Her eyes flashed. "Don't you believe me? It was Mr. Demsky and . . ."

Cal's father tugged on her sleeve. "Come on, Cal. We need to go."

"Don't touch me!" Cal snapped.

Her father's hand fell away. "I'm so sorry," he mumbled to Mrs. Demsky and Paloma. "With Elaine . . . and everything . . ."

"There's no need to apologize," Mrs. Demsky said.

Cal gave the room one more glance before pushing past her father. She ran down Mountain Road.

This time, her dad kept up. "Cal, you're exhausted and probably dehydrated. Let's go home. You need food and—"

"I don't want you here!" she yelled at him as she sloshed through puddles.

She kept going until she couldn't hear his footsteps

any longer. A stitch grew in her side until it hurt so much, she had to stop. She leaned over, gasping for air. When she stood, she saw that she was in front of Demsky's Market. A cardboard CLOSED sign hung in the window.

"I guess you think you're pretty funny, Mr. Demsky?" she shouted. "What, is this another one of your tricks?"

The only answer was the pounding rain.

She turned to face the mountain. With no sun, the spire remained as dark and empty as if it wore a CLOSED sign too.

She cradled her bruised elbow, trying to separate fact from fiction. Science from faith.

The rain tapered and a breeze swirled—as soft and gentle as a whisper. She closed her eyes and, for a second, thought she heard a voice.

Everything is as it should be.

Cal exhaled all the air she'd been holding inside, as if those mysterious words, or the rain, or Mr. Demsky himself had put out her angry flames.

She looked up the road. There was Dad, hands in his pockets, rain dripping down his face. He hadn't let her out of his sight the whole time.

Cal took a deep breath, then slogged back up the road. When she reached him, she kept walking.

He followed her, past the broken shutter, up the steps, and into their house.

Inside, she immediately found the fist-size black hole.

Her father stared at it with her. "I'm sorry that's still there. I need to get some spackle and paint to repair it."

Cal's gaze remained fixed on the hole.

"You must be starving," he said. "How about some tomato soup and a grilled cheese?"

Cal nodded. Rain pooled in puddles by her feet.

"Why don't you take a hot shower and change into warm clothes?" He walked into the kitchen and grabbed a skillet.

She took a step, then paused. With her right hand, she cupped her left fist. Remembering.

Her father put down the pan and walked toward her. He raised his arms as if he wanted to hug her but couldn't remember how to.

"I'm going to go take that shower now," she said.

"Okay. Food will be ready when you are."

Cal traced the edge of the black hole with her fingertip. Then she went inside her room and closed the door.

Chapter 23

The next morning, Cal sat on her bed fully dressed.
There was a knock.

"Come in."

Her bedroom door creaked open. It was Dad. He wore
a crisp blue dress shirt tucked into pressed jeans. He
pushed up his glasses, and Cal noticed that the tape was
gone. "I'm leaving for the hospital. Jorge Lopez is bringing me. Are you sure you don't want to come?"

"Mr. Lopez?" Of course, they were climbing friends.
It was just weird, since he was older than her father . . .
and also her teacher.

"Yeah." Dad nodded. "He's the only other person who

visited me besides you and Mom. He's been a real friend through . . ." He paused. "Everything."

Her father dug his hands in his pockets. "Mom would really like to see you, Cal. I—I mean, she may be asleep the whole time, but you know Mom." He tried to smile. "She'll know you're there."

An image of Mom from early Saturday morning popped into Cal's head. She'd been so pale. Murmuring in her sleep. The guilt of that moment fell on Cal all over again. Heavy as a boulder.

Cal shook her head.

"I think it would help if you came."

Dad was lying. Cal knew she'd already failed at the one thing that could have helped her mother. *There is no such thing as magic*, she wanted to say. Instead, she stared out the window.

Her dad cleared his throat. "Look, Cal, I know you've been through a lot, but . . ." He sniffed. "What you did was not okay."

Cal had told him about camping on the landing, but she hadn't told him that they were searching for the magic, or that she and Rosine had scaled the spire. She knew he wouldn't understand.

A red Jeep pulled up.

"And leaving that note about going to Viola's . . . Do you have any idea how terrified we all were when we realized you weren't there? Viola was beside herself." Dad's voice cracked. "Promise me you'll never do something like that again."

"I won't," Cal said. But she didn't mean that she wouldn't run off again. She just meant that she'd never be so foolish as to think she had the power to change anything.

Dad nodded as if he understood.

Cal stifled a sob, because she knew he never would.

The Jeep tooted.

Dad glanced out the window, then back at Cal. "That's Lopez." He took a deep breath. "Okay, I won't force you to come with me."

Good, she thought, *because I'm not going anyway.*

"But I'm not leaving you home without any supervision either. I already called Paloma, in case you weren't going. She'll be checking in on you a little later this morning."

"No." Cal swung her legs over the side of the bed and sat up. "I don't need a babysitter." Really, she was embarrassed about how she'd acted at the Demskys' the day before.

"Sorry. Nonnegotiable."

Cal looked out the window, thinking, *She can't check on me if I'm not here.*

"I have to go now, but we're not finished talking about this." He sniffed. "Call me on my cell if you need anything." He paused. "And, Cal . . ."

She looked up.

"I love you, sweetheart." He leaned forward as if he were going to try to hug her again.

She crossed her arms.

"Okay," he said. Then he left.

She heard the front door shut. Through the window she watched him climb into the Jeep. It turned around and rumbled down Mountain Road.

Cal pulled her knees up and hugged them. She could barely stand the stillness. It made her feel as if her insides were jumbled. Nothing was right . . . and without the dream of finding the magic meteorite, she had no idea how to fix it anymore.

As much as Cal wanted to see her mom, she knew she wasn't strong enough to face her.

I'm weak, she thought. *I've always been weak.* Right then, she couldn't remember a time when she'd ever felt strong.

Then she did.

It was on the spire.

When she'd decided to face its challenge.

She never would've made it that far without Rosine.

Rosine was the strongest person Cal had ever met. Being near her was enough to make Cal feel brave too. It was as if Rosine's courage was contagious.

Cal had an idea. What if facing Mom's illness was like facing the mountain? She couldn't do it alone, but she *could* if Rosine came with her.

She looked at her alarm clock. Eight A.M. She stood up.

It was still early, but she couldn't wait. She had to see Rosine.

She walked into the kitchen and grabbed her mom's jacket from its hook and threw it on. Then she yanked open the front door.

"Hey."

Cal blinked.

Rosine stood on the front step holding her purple backpack. "Um, can I come in?" she asked.

"Oh, yeah. Yes. Of course." Cal opened the door wide. "Come in—come inside." She wasn't sure why she suddenly felt awkward. "I was actually just coming to see you."

Rosine handed Cal the backpack.

"Why are you—" Cal began, then she realized the bag

was squirming. "Wildcat!" She placed the bag on the kitchen table and carefully lifted Wildcat out.

He looked up at her with sleepy eyes, purring softly as if to say, *Okay. Stop crying. You're getting my fur wet.*

"He's very sore and needs to rest, but Mali says he'll be fine."

Cal buried her face in Wildcat's fur, letting his deep purr vibrate into her heart.

"Mali says to make a warm bed for him and put a bowl of water nearby but no food for now. The most important thing is to let him sleep."

Cal looked at Rosine. "Thank you," she said. "You and Mali. You saved Wildcat."

Rosine shrugged. "It was Mali, really."

"I need your help, Rosine. Again, I mean." She took a deep breath. "My mom is in the hospital, and she's going to have that surgery, and I know I should go see her . . . I mean I *want* to see her, but . . ."

Rosine shifted.

"The thing is, I need you to make me strong enough to go there. To . . . I don't know . . . face whatever . . ." She bit her lip. "I can't do it without you."

"I'm sorry, Cal. I can't do that."

"What? Why? It won't be long . . . and . . . I have to find us a ride, but—"

"We're leaving, Cal."

"What?"

Rosine hugged herself. "Mali and I are going to Hartford today. Mrs. Demsky is bringing us to the bus station soon."

Cal spun away, finding the black hole. She stared into it.

"The truth is, Cal, you don't need me. You're already brave."

Cal bit her lip. "No, I'm not."

The girls stood in silence.

"There's something else," Rosine finally said, "that I need to tell you."

"What?"

"You were right. I did lie to you."

"What do you mean?"

"The wooden box. I took it."

Cal felt tears poke the corners of her eyes.

"But I didn't steal it," Rosine continued. "It was mine. The word sewn into the cloth—*amani*—my mother sewed that. It was from a song she used to sing to me."

Cal thought back to when she first discovered the box. The way it had been so intricately carved, she'd known right away that it was special. She remembered sounding out the word *amani* and how it felt on her tongue.

Her eyes locked with Rosine's. "It *was* you . . . the singing. I heard you when I was outside the Demskys' house."

Rosine nodded. "Yes. 'Amani.' My mother always sang this song to us. But it was more than that. It was something she wanted Mali and I to find for ourselves." She took a deep breath. "Before she died my mother told me, *Rosine, when you find the perfect place—a magical place— put this box there and know I will always be with you.*"

"But . . . why the spire?" Cal asked.

"I told you that the mountain reminded me of home. From the moment I came to this town, I went exploring there. Right away I felt . . . I don't know . . . different when I was there. Better. I knew it was a special place. When I found the cave, I thought my mother's box would be safe there. Then, when you talked about it in Mr. Demsky's shop, I knew I had to move the box, so I followed you there that afternoon."

"You took it back the next day," Cal said.

"Yes, when I went alone to feed Wildcat. By then I knew the spire was where I needed to leave the box." Rosine said, "That day with Mr. Demsky, I could tell that you believed in the magic. That was enough for me." Rosine paused. "When we made it to the top of the spire, I knew the magic was real. I could feel it."

In her mind's eye, Cal was transported back to the spire's peak with its soda pop air and the feeling of being on top of the world.

"But the box . . . it's like a memory of your mother. Why would you leave it there?"

"That's the difference between you and me, Cal. You think you have to hold on to something to keep it. I know that the opposite is true."

Cal shook her head. "I don't understand."

"My mother is always with me, Cal. I don't need a wooden box to know that." Rosine took a deep breath. "Mr. Demsky was right, you know?"

"About the meteorite?"

"About the magic." She laughed.

Cal frowned. She felt her throat closing, the way it always did when she was trying hard not to cry. She still didn't understand what Rosine was telling her. But even worse was the fact that Rosine hadn't trusted her.

"Why didn't you tell me?" Cal asked. "I would have understood."

"Would you have?"

Cal sighed. "No. Not then."

Even though it had only been a couple of days since they'd scaled the spire, it felt like a lifetime ago. Everything had changed.

"I'm glad you told me now," Cal said.

Rosine dug her hands in her pockets. "I almost forgot. I have something else for you." She held up a small glass jar filled with gravel.

"The dirt you took from the spire."

Rosine grinned. "If you want to see dirt, then that's what you'll see . . . but if you believe in magic . . ."

"That's what you'll find," Cal whispered.

"I'm sorry, Cal, but I really have to go." She reached for the doorknob.

Watching Rosine walk out of her life felt something like losing a part of her insides. She needed to do something, anything, to make her stay. "I lied too," Cal blurted.

Rosine paused.

Cal walked to the wall and faced the black hole. With her left hand, she formed a fist and put it inside. It was a perfect fit.

"You punched the wall?"

"My arm didn't break in the car accident. I broke it the day the police came to arrest my dad for the accident . . ." The tears she'd been holding back began to stream down her face. She didn't bother to wipe them away.

"That's over, Cal. Do you hear me?" Rosine's eyes were fierce. "You are not that girl anymore."

Cal wanted to believe Rosine. She wanted to be more like her.

"I can't face my mom without you, Rosine." Through Cal's tears, everything appeared wobbly and distorted.

"Remember when we were on the peak and we were still connected by the rope?" Rosine asked. "Even when I couldn't see you, I knew you were there because I could feel you tugging on me."

Cal put a hand to her waist.

"There will always be a rope between us, Cal, whether you can see it or not. And whenever you feel as if you're going to fall, all you need to do is tie a knot and hold on." She shrugged. "Because I'll be holding the other end." Rosine opened the door and stepped outside. "Goodbye, Cal."

Cal looked at her feet.

"Aren't you going to say goodbye?"

"No," she whispered.

"Okay," Rosine said. "I understand." Then she closed the door behind her.

Chapter 24

Cal took deep breaths as she stared at the jar of dirt in her hand. For some reason her brain flashed back to the massive oak tree struck by lightning. Right then she knew exactly how that tree must have felt when ni umeme had split it in two.

Her heart felt the same way.

She shoved the jar of dirt in the pocket of her mom's jacket she was still wearing, then stared at the fist-size black hole.

Watching her father being led out of their home in handcuffs when Mom was still so sick had made her feel more out of control than any other time in her life. More than when she found out about Mom's cancer, even more than when the car slid off the road.

That day had become *the day when everything changed*, because it was the day Cal had changed.

It was the day she'd let fear take over.

Then Cal met Rosine, and she felt herself changing again. Not back to the Cal she'd been, but into a new Cal.

Fear still whispered in her ear, but since the spire, instead of hiding from it, she'd learned to face it.

Wildcat gave a soft purr. Cal picked him up and brought him into her room. She placed him gently on the bed so he could see his mountain through the window.

Cal watched his chest rise and fall. He'd been shaved where the stitches were, and there weren't any dead leaves or sticks in his fur. She thought about how angry he must have been when he woke up to find himself clean.

"You're okay," Cal whispered. "You're still Wildcat. The one and only."

She went into the kitchen and grabbed a bowl. She filled it with water and carefully brought it back to her room.

As she placed it on the floor, she said, "I'm going to go for a walk, Wildcat."

He stretched and yawned before curling in a ball. Soon he was purring the deep sounds of sleep.

Cal left, shutting the door behind her. Outside, the cold, raw air immediately filled her lungs, making her cough. She zipped up the jacket, smelling Mom's lilac perfume on the collar. It was only mid-October, but the promise of snow filled the air.

At the end of her driveway, she nodded at the mountain. Then she headed down the road. She didn't know where she was going, but the cold felt so good against her hot cheeks that she didn't care.

The scent of decaying leaves and burning firewood filled the air. She listened for the crickets' song, but the only sound came from the rattle of dried leaves as they skittered across the pavement.

When she reached the corner of Mountain Road and Main Street, she wondered where to go next. She glanced at Demsky's Market, realizing there was a light on. She walked up the steps. The CLOSED sign was still in the window, but someone was inside.

The door popped open.

Cal jumped back in surprise.

"Cal Scott! I thought that was you," Paloma said. Her long brown hair was pulled back in a ponytail, but a few strands had fallen out. She wore a T-shirt that read GO

BLUE! Mr. Demsky's long white apron was tied around her waist.

"I was about to head up to your house," Paloma said. "But since you're here, would you like to come in?"

"Okay." Cal stepped inside. For a moment she wondered where she was, because this place didn't look anything like the Demsky's Market she knew.

The dusty floors were clean and polished. Shelves of food and supplies had been tidied and rearranged. The entire market seemed brighter.

"It smells like . . ." Cal sniffed. "Lemons and fresh-cut grass."

"Do you like it? I think this place was ready for a deep clean, huh?" Paloma laughed. "I'm so glad you're here, Cal. I wanted to talk to you."

Cal jammed her fists in her pockets. "I—I'm sorry . . . ," she began.

Paloma picked up a broom. "No, no, don't be."

The two stared hard at each other.

"I want you to know that I believe you . . . about seeing Pop," Paloma finally said. "I believe you because he visited me too."

"You do? He did?"

"Yeah. He was wearing that old blue flannel shirt with the hole in the elbow that my mother kept throwing out, but he somehow kept finding . . ." She shook her head. "And his apron from work." She smoothed the long white apron wrapped around her waist.

"He was?"

"You know"—Paloma nodded—"that's exactly something Pop would do. Head to the mountain he loved."

"When you saw him, did he say anything?" Cal asked.

"Nope. He didn't have to. I needed to see that he was okay, and I knew right then that he was." She sighed. "I'd been asleep and then—all of a sudden—he was there, right in front of me. At first, I thought I was dreaming. He put his hand on my forehead, and I kind of woke up. Then he disappeared again."

Tears sprang to Cal's eyes. She'd been feeling so bad for herself, and here Paloma had just lost her father. "I'm so sorry."

"Don't be." Paloma smiled, but her eyes were wet too. She began sweeping. "Now, tell me," she said. "What were you doing on the mountain in a storm?"

Even though Cal hadn't told her dad the whole truth, somehow she knew that Paloma would understand. "Rosine and I climbed the spire," she finally said.

Paloma stopped sweeping. "That's amazing!"

Cal fought an outside smile. "It was your father who

made me want to do it. You know, his stories of the magic meteorite."

"Oh, I know." Paloma began sweeping again. "He tried to get me to go with him, but I'm not much of a climber. Tell me what it's like up there."

Cal thought back to that first dizzying moment. How the soda pop air sparkled around her and electricity coursed through her veins.

"The best part was how it made me feel."

"What was that like?"

"It's hard to explain. At first, I had so many feelings . . . like, swishing around inside me. I had dreamed of climbing the spire for so long, and . . ." She met Paloma's gaze. "I did it. It was really hard, but . . . we made it." She nodded slowly. "And when I got there, somehow, I knew that was supposed to happen, you know? Like I was exactly where I was supposed to be." She bit her lip, letting her gaze fall to the floor. "At first anyway. Then I ruined everything."

"You did? How?"

"Because I was so worried about finding the meteorite, I didn't take time to . . . I don't know . . . enjoy the moment. I mean, we'd pulled off this amazing climb . . . We were on top of the spire . . . but all I could see was what wasn't there instead of what was."

Paloma nodded. After a moment she asked, "So, what does it look like up there?"

"There's a huge boulder that I'm pretty sure is milky quartz."

"That sounds right," Paloma said. "That's probably what the sun is hitting when it begins to set—you know, that makes the spire look as though it's on fire."

"Oh yeah," Cal said. "I never thought of that." She frowned. She'd wanted to believe it was the magic meteorite creating that light show.

Cal continued, "The top of the spire is definitely bigger than it looks from here, and it's pretty flat with a lot of, like, grayish gravel."

"So, no magic meteorite?"

Cal shook her head. "Definitely no magic meteorite."

"Hmmmm, well, you know, I'm a mineralogist, but I'm not sure you knew that my main focus is the study of micrometeorites—also known as stardust."

"Your dad told us that."

"I have my own theory."

"About the spire?"

"About the meteorite. And why no one's found evidence that one landed there."

"Really?" Cal said. "What?"

"Often, when a meteoroid enters the atmosphere, it

sublimates, or turns from solid directly to a gas, leaving nothing behind." She shrugged. "Other times, it enters the atmosphere in dust particles. Thousands of tons of cosmic dust fall on the earth each year. What I'm trying to say is that just because no one's found a meteorite on the mountain doesn't mean there wasn't a meteor."

"Even a green meteor?"

"Green meteors are not uncommon. The color of light that the meteors produce depends on their chemical composition. A meteor made mostly of calcium will appear purple, iron will appear yellow, nitrogen and oxygen—red. Also, the speed of the meteor can affect the intensity of the color. The faster the meteor moves, the more vibrant the color. The green Pop saw tells us that meteor was likely composed of magnesium or nickel."

Cal thought about that. Although it was interesting, it was also disappointing. All this time she was looking for something that had probably never existed in the first place. "Have you ever found stardust?"

Paloma nodded. "Of course. Stardust is everywhere. If you want to learn more about it, I can lend you books by Carl Sagan, Neil deGrasse Tyson, and Jon Larsen."

"What do they say?"

"We are made of stardust."

Cal rolled her eyes. "That's something you hear on cheesy TV shows."

"I guess. But that doesn't mean it's not true. Are you familiar with the periodic table of elements?"

Cal nodded, thinking back to her oganesson element that ended up being helium.

"Most elements were created in stars via stellar nucleosynthesis or supernovae that happened billions of years ago. These events sent tons of stardust containing the elements that ultimately created life on earth into the universe. If it weren't for stardust, none of us would be here."

"I guess Mr. Lopez was right, then. He had a different theory, but the same result. It's not magic. It's science."

"If that's how you want to look at it."

"Yeah, because that's the way it is."

"Well, if you ask me, the two go hand in hand. Every scientist recognizes that there are events—forces and powers—that absolutely exist but no one can explain."

"Like what?"

"Like talking to someone who passed away three days earlier."

Cal's hand immediately felt for the egg-shaped bruise on her elbow.

"Stardust is real, Cal. And that's a fact. Whether it's magical or not? Well, that's up to you."

"If you want to see a rock, that's all you'll see . . ."

"If you believe in magic, then that's what you'll find," Paloma finished. "Pop used to say that." She picked up the broom again. "Maybe someday you can teach me how to climb, and we'll scale the spire together. I'd love to collect samples from there to study."

Cal reached into her pocket and held up the jar of dirt. "You mean like this?"

The broom dropped.

"No way," Paloma said, accepting the jar. "That's from the spire?"

Cal nodded. "Rosine collected it."

"Come on!" Paloma said, heading to the back.

As Cal followed Paloma into Mr. Demsky's office, she noticed it had been cleaned too. The floors and shelves glistened. The rocks that had been piled on the desk were gone. Cheery blue curtains replaced the blinds and showed off sparkling clean windows. The pile of old black-and-white photos now hung on the wall, neat and straight.

Paloma sat down at the table with her father's microscope. She poured a few grains of the dirt onto a slide and put it under the lens. "Check it out," she said.

When Cal looked through the eyepiece, she saw that what had looked like a few ordinary grains, under magnification now appeared spherical—like tiny glass balls. Most of them were black, but one had a slight green tinge to it.

"Is that stardust?" she asked.

"I can't tell for sure, but it's very cool, isn't it?"

Cal nodded.

"Manmade or terrestrial spherules are pretty common, especially since there was once a factory nearby. But the fact that they appear so round is promising, and the greenish one looks like olivine. That is the most common mineral in micrometeorites."

"Wow," Cal said. "But again . . . it's science, not magic."

"Are you kidding? Think about it, Cal. That speck of dust could be billions of years old. It could have come from star explosions that enriched the galaxy in heavy elements that ultimately formed our solar system. The atoms in your body were actually forged inside a star. When we look at stardust, or into the universe for that matter, we're really looking back at ourselves. What could be more magical than that?"

Paloma was saying so much . . . stuff. The information was too much to think about all at once. Cal wanted to tuck each piece away so she could figure it out like a puzzle—piece by piece.

"You know my dad liked to quote Neil deGrasse Tyson.

One of his favorites was about how each of us really is a little universe."

"Yeah, he told me and Rosine that."

Paloma bit her lip. "I don't know why I remembered that right now. I guess looking through his microscope . . ." She peered inside the eyepiece again. "Seeing something that may have been created billions of years ago in a cosmic explosion . . . that traveled all that time and distance to find us here at Demsky's Market. I don't know. It reminds me that we are all connected to the universe."

"And to each other," Cal said.

"Definitely," Paloma said. "I'd really like to send these in for analysis. Would that be okay?"

"Will I get it back?"

"Nope, sorry. But it could be important for science."

Cal thought about it. "Rosine would like that."

As Paloma carefully set aside the sample, Cal looked around the office, admiring Paloma's work.

"Are you getting this place ready to sell or something?"

Paloma hugged herself. "Oh no, I could never sell Demsky's Market. There's too much of Pop here."

"But you're a scientist. How will you have time to run a market too?"

"Actually, I have an idea. Want to hear it?"

"Sure."

Paloma leaned in. "You probably don't know this, but during COVID, when the factory closed and people were out of work, Pop stopped taking money from customers who needed food and other items but were short on cash."

Cal remembered what Mr. Demsky had told her mom. *Help yourself to whatever you need, Elaine.*

"Of course, it wasn't just Pop. Lots of neighbors contributed. Some people baked bread, or canned fruit, or even sewed face masks."

Cal thought back to the afternoon she'd seen the Misses stocking jars of peaches. She had wondered why they were putting jars onto shelves instead of into their cart. Now she knew.

"Pop always believed that difficult situations were a lot easier to face with a friend by your side. Really, he dedicated his life to that idea," Paloma said. "So, I thought I'd officially make this place what it already is. I'm going to turn Demsky's Market into a community food pantry. Mom's already agreed to help, and Abner too." She looked around the office. "I've cleaned things up, but I want to make this space bigger and continue my research here. Hearing about your experience on the spire gives me even more reason to believe this is the perfect place for me."

"After traveling the world, you're going to move back to Bleakerville?"

Paloma looked around and nodded. "Yeah. You bet I am." She grinned.

"Wow. That's so cool. I mean—all of it." Cal blinked. "Are you still going to call it Demsky's Market?" For some reason, that didn't seem right anymore.

"Hmm. I was hoping to come up with a new name. Any ideas?"

Cal shook her head. "No, but I'll think about it."

Paloma picked up a duster. "Since I have you here, do you mind if I finish up a few things before I bring you home?"

"Sure, um, I can help." Cal began to follow Paloma back into the market, then froze. One of the photos Paloma had hung caught her eye.

She studied it carefully. It was the black-and-white one of two men dressed in baggy climbing clothes and standing on either side of a white boulder. "No way!" Cal exclaimed.

"No way, what?" Paloma asked.

Cal squinted. "This photo was taken on top of the spire," she said.

Paloma looked at it. "I don't think so." She pointed at the man with the dark, bushy mustache. "That's Pop."

"Mr. Demsky?" He was so young in the photo Cal hadn't recognized him.

"Are you sure it's the spire?" Paloma asked.

"I know it is. I was there." She pointed to the white boulder. "That's the milky quartz I told you about. We used that rock as an anchor to rappel down." She shook her head. "Mr. Demsky . . . and this other guy . . . they must have been the scientists who reached the peak . . . and then disappeared. They had to be!"

Paloma examined the photo. "My father never told me he'd climbed the spire."

Suddenly Cal wanted to find Rosine so she could tell her.

"Well, I'll be." Paloma shook her head. "I wonder why Pop never told me." She looked closer. "I don't know who that other man is."

The other climber appeared younger than Mr. Demsky. He had dark eyes, and his hair was thick and black. The image was grainy, but when Cal looked hard, she noticed something else. While Mr. Demsky grinned straight into the camera, the other man seemed lost in thought. His left arm wrapped across his waist while he pinched his chin with his right hand.

"My mother can probably tell you who that is," Paloma said, walking back into the storefront. "Anyway, would you mind wiping down the shelves and restocking them? There's a fresh cloth and disinfectant over there."

Cal followed Paloma and grabbed the cleaning supplies. Paloma handed her a box marked FOR AISLE 3. Cal set it down and began cleaning. A million thoughts rushed through her head as she worked to puzzle out the photo and what it meant.

She opened the box and lifted a can. As she set it on the shelf, she blinked. It was a bright yellow tin of sardines.

A tingle ran up her spine.

Paloma walked past and must have misread her reaction because she laughed. "I know. I'm not a canned fish fan either, but some people love them."

Cal set it on the shelf, thinking about everything that had happened in the last few days.

It had all begun with a yellow tin of sardines.

Mr. Demsky could have scolded her when he discovered she'd taken it. He could have called her mother , , , or the police even. Instead, he took Cal and Rosine into his office and talked about mountains and magic and facing the impossible. He brought them together.

As Cal stacked the cans, she watched Paloma scurry about. Even though Mr. Demsky was no longer there, it was clear his daughter felt his presence inside this place he loved.

Maybe it was like that for Rosine too. Except by leaving her mother's memory on the mountain, she was able to feel her mom's presence everywhere.

Rosine had faced her impossibles.

Maybe it's time for me to face mine, Cal thought.

She touched her hand to her waist as if she could feel a tug. She knew Rosine wouldn't physically be by her side. She also knew she'd be there just the same.

At that very moment, Mr. Demsky's voice seemed to fill her head. *Everything is as it should be.*

The voice was so clear—so real—that Cal turned to see if Paloma had heard it too. She watched her put the duster down and turn to gaze at Mount Meteorite.

"Paloma?" Cal whispered.

"Yes?" she said without turning from the mountain.

"Instead of home, can you give me a ride somewhere else?"

"Where to?" Paloma asked.

"Memorial Hospital?"

Paloma's eyes were still wet with tears. "You bet I can," she said.

Chapter 25

On the way to the hospital, Paloma called Cal's dad to let him know they were coming. "I have to get home to be with my mother," she said as Cal got out of the car. "Your dad said he'd meet you inside, and Mr. Lopez will bring you both home."

"Thanks, Paloma," Cal said. "For everything."

"Of course. I'll see you soon."

Cal nodded. When she reached the hospital's front entrance, a large glass door slid open. She stepped inside and came to a long desk. Behind it, doctors and nurses wearing scrubs and white jackets rushed in every direction. Other men and women pushed wheelchairs and stretchers.

Cal didn't know where to go.

"Can I help you?" A gray-haired woman wearing a blue smock approached her.

"I'm here to see my mom. She's a patient. My father's here too . . . somewhere."

"What's your mom here for?"

"She has cancer . . . She's here for a surgery."

"What's her name?"

"Elaine Scott."

The woman checked her tablet. "She is in the north wing." She handed Cal a sticker that read VISITOR and a paper mask. "Put these on and go to the eighth floor." She pointed to a row of elevators.

Cal walked over and got inside. She hugged herself, wondering where her father was.

When the elevator dinged, she stepped out. In front of her was a desk, but no one was at it. She walked past it to see a long white corridor lined with doors, one after the other.

A tingle ran up her spine.

Cal slowly walked down the hallway. She could hear people in the rooms, but the doors were closed, except for the one at the very end of the corridor. As much as she didn't want to go there, she felt it pull her toward it like a magnet.

Although she didn't feel her feet moving, she seemed to be drawing closer and closer to the open door as if caught in a river's current.

When there was nowhere left to go, she stepped inside the room.

At first, Cal didn't recognize her mom lying on the hospital bed. There were bags of clear liquid hanging from a metal stand and tubes that ran into the back of each hand.

There was a machine with numbers that kept changing and squiggly lines that went up and down, up and down.

Her mother was dressed in a hospital gown that was so large it seemed to swallow her up. There was a chair next to the bed and a little table with a pink pitcher and a glass of water.

Cal slipped into the chair. "Hi, Mom," she said.

Her mother didn't budge.

She watched the heart monitor—*lub dub, lub dub, lub dub.*

"I wanted to let you know that I'm sorry I left without telling you," Cal took a deep breath, and continued, "I went to climb Mount Meteorite."

Her mother's chest rose and fell.

"It's okay if you want to ground me. I get it." Cal almost

smiled. "But . . . I want you to know I made it, Mom. Rosine and me . . . we summited the spire."

She looked at her mother's hands, taped and bandaged.

"The whole way up, there were . . . lots of problems. First, there was this bear, but don't worry, he was more scared of us than we were of him, like you've always told me." She sighed. "And then we lost our water . . . but Rosine got more. My boots got wet, so we shared a pair. I wouldn't recommend that."

Cal sniffed. "But we got to the landing and built a shelter and a fire, and we cooked beans right in the can. Mom, they were the best beans I've ever had in my whole life."

She studied her mother's frail shape beneath the blankets.

"But you know what I really figured out on the mountain, Mom? All those people who said it was impossible to summit the spire—well, they were looking at it from far away." She paused, staring into her mother's face. "When I got up close and really studied it like Dad always does, I saw that it was totally possible," she said. "So, I kept going and studying and . . . finding new paths until I reached the top."

Cal's forehead wrinkled. "It made me think of . . . you know, our situation. I've been looking at everything from far away, and that's made it all seem pretty impossible. But if we look at it up close, and if we examine it carefully and take on each problem one at a time, I think we can find our path forward too."

Cal took a deep breath. "The other thing, I guess, that really helped Rosine and me is that we never gave up. Even when we faced all those problems." She sighed. "Rosine taught me that, Mom. She's, like, the superhero of never giving up."

An image flashed across Cal's brain. Rosine in her green hoodie, standing on the front step.

Rosine saying goodbye.

And Cal not saying goodbye back, as if that would have made her stay.

No matter what Cal said or didn't say. No matter what she did or didn't do. Rosine was still gone.

But was she?

Cal touched a hand to her waist and for a millisecond felt a tug—as if the rope were still there and Rosine were on the other end.

She thought about Rosine going back for the gravel, but then giving it to her.

Cal knew Rosine didn't take it because she thought it was magic. She took it because she wanted to remember that place—the struggle to get there, and the way they'd felt when they reached the top. It's why she'd left the intricate box and its carefully stitched word there, too. There was a lot more than just dirt in that bottle. It was a symbol of who they were and what they'd done.

The dirt was part of the mountain the same way they were.

Cal knew right then that the magic had never been something that could be found on the mountain, because it was already inside them.

Maybe it wasn't the kind of magic that she'd been looking for. But it was definitely the kind she needed.

Cal stood up and put a hand on her mother's arm.

Mom's eyelids fluttered.

"No matter what happens, Mom," Cal said, "I'm going to be okay. Dad too. We're going to be okay together." She nodded. "I'm still not saying goodbye, but I want you to know . . ." Cal's throat began to ache. "What I *need* you to know, Mom, is that I totally believe in the magic." She fought through her tears. "I believe in the magic of us."

Cal heard a noise. She turned to see her father standing in the doorway, his hands in his pockets. Tears streamed down his face.

Cal fixed her gaze on his. "All of us."

She turned back to Mom and kissed her on the forehead. "No more nightmares," she whispered.

Then she walked to her dad and buried her face in his shirt. Even in that airless room, he smelled like the mountain. "I missed you so much," she said.

As her father wrapped his arms tightly around her, she could hear his muffled reply. "I told you, sweetheart. I'm never letting go."

Chapter 26

On the drive home, Cal stared at the back of Mr. Lopez's head. She had so many things she wanted to ask him but was unsure where to start. Finally, she couldn't hold it in anymore. Even though so much had changed in the past few days, some things had stayed the same—Cal's mouth and words still had a mind of their own.

"I know the truth about Mount Meteorite," she said.

"What do you mean, Cal?" her dad asked.

"Mr. Lopez knows what I mean." She addressed him directly. "Right, Mr. Lopez? You told us one thing in school, but I think you believe something totally different, because you were there."

Mr. Lopez kept driving, but in the rearview mirror she could see he was grinning.

"Cal, what are you talking about? Show Mr. Lopez some respect. He's your teacher, after all."

"Tell him, Mr. Lopez. Tell my dad that you were one of the scientists to summit the spire. I know it because I saw the photo of you standing on its peak next to the milky-quartz boulder."

Mr. Lopez slapped the steering wheel. "I can't believe it, Scott. You did it!"

"She did what?" Cal's dad spun around, facing her. "You did what, Cal?"

"Scott scaled the spire."

"Sorry, Dad, I was going to tell you."

"You told me you camped on the landing. You never said anything about the spire."

"It was fine, Dad," Cal said, knowing it kind of wasn't. "I was with Rosine, and I did everything you taught me. Really, it was like you were there too."

Dad buried his face in his hands. "Don't . . . please don't ever do that again." He peeked through his fingers. "Unless we do it together."

"I promise," Cal said.

After a moment, she continued, "You know what else you were wrong about, Mr. Lopez?"

"I have a feeling you're going to tell me."

"There *is* magic. I'm sure of it now."

"I know that's what Demsky wanted everyone to believe." He shook a finger in the air. "But I am a scientist. I am a man of fact."

"Maybe you can be both," her father offered.

Cal thought about what Paloma had said. She was a scientist, yet she had faith in the unproven—the impossible, even. *The two go hand in hand*, she'd said.

"Mr. Lopez, why didn't you tell me you'd climbed the spire?" Cal asked. "Why did you say the scientists disappeared when you were one of them? Why didn't you tell anyone what you saw?"

"Cal—" her father began.

Mr. Lopez shook his head, still grinning. "It's perfectly fine. Your daughter asks important questions. And she deserves answers."

"Okay," her father said, crossing his arms. "I don't even know what you two are talking about, but I'd like to hear also."

Cal was pretty sure that if Mr. Lopez hadn't been driving, he'd have crossed an arm across his waist and pinched his chin with the other hand.

"First off, I never said any of that. It was your classmates and others who claimed it was impossible. Not me. Also, I never said what happened to the scientists except that they weren't heard from again—and we weren't. As far as the spire was concerned, anyway."

"I don't understand," Cal said. "How did you wind up scaling the spire with Mr. Demsky?"

"I told you he was once my professor—one of my favorites, in fact. He knew I was a climber and wrangled me into joining him that February morning. We both set out with open minds. Neither of us had ever been to Bleakerville before, and when we stopped for coffee in town, Demsky told the shopkeeper what we were up to. I guess he then, in turn, told the whole town. It wasn't until many years later, when Demsky moved here, that we learned they'd been waiting for us to descend so we could tell them what we'd seen. We must have left sooner than they thought we would, and we missed each other. Apparently, they went looking for us, but only found our equipment. The rest of the story grew from there."

"Did you find *anything* on the summit?"

"When we reached the top of the spire, Demsky and I couldn't agree on what we were looking at. He kept talking about the *heavenly green light he'd seen,* and the magic he felt." Mr. Lopez shrugged. "For me, it was like most other climbs. Lovely, but gravelly and quite gray.

"On the way down, Demsky wouldn't stop talking about how certain he was that a *spiritual* event had occurred." Mr. Lopez shook his head. "The problem was, he had no proof. There was no meteorite, no crater. There was nothing there. Ultimately, we agreed to disagree.

"We stored our gear in a remote cave. It was our way of promising each other that when we'd proved our respective theories, we'd return to the summit." Mr. Lopez raised his eyebrows. "But we never did."

"What happened?" Cal asked.

"Life happened." Mr. Lopez sighed. "Demsky started a family. I continued my research and began teaching." He nodded. "I pursued practical routes—while Demsky never seemed to get his head out of the clouds. There was a time we discussed heading back up, but then decided not to."

"Why?"

"We realized it didn't matter."

"What do you mean?"

"Demsky saw magic in everything, that's the way he was. He always did his best to promote his theory, and the legend grew and grew." He shook his head. "I'm a science guy at heart. Sorry, but I saw what I saw. In the end, we decided to leave the gear there for the next scientists ready to resolve the questions we left unanswered."

"Rosine and me."

Mr. Lopez nodded. "You know, Scott, the only reason I gave you a hard time when you asked me if I thought you couldn't scale the spire was because I knew that would make you want to try. I've seen you climb. I know what you can do. But"—he turned briefly, catching Cal's eye—"I meant for you to try with your dad or me ... not on your own!"

"I wasn't alone. I had Rosine."

"You know what I mean."

The Jeep was silent as they got off the interstate.

"So, do you see that Mr. Demsky was right now?" Cal asked.

"That's the point, Cal. It's not about being right or wrong. For Demsky, it was a matter of faith. For me, it was a matter of proof. We each had our own hypothesis. Until someone proves things one way or the other, I'm not going to change my mind."

"But that's not an answer at all."

"Welcome to science, Cal. Sometimes there is no answer. That's what scientists are here for ... to keep asking questions. To keep searching for the truth." He sighed. "But I'll tell you this. What I teach in class is scientific principle. I want you to make hypotheses and then prove them, not the other way around. Even so, it's important to remember that discovering the science behind a miracle doesn't make it less magical. Personally, I think the opposite is true."

"Paloma said the same thing."

"I'm sure she got that from her father too." Mr. Lopez said. "I guess what I'm trying to say is that no matter what I believe and how much I rely on fact, I've always been jealous of Demsky. I've wondered what it would be like to . . ." He let his words drift off.

"To what?"

But Mr. Lopez let her question hang in the air, instead fixing his gaze on Cal in the rearview mirror. "You really did it, Scott. You summited the spire!"

Cal nodded.

Mr. Lopez shook his head, laughing. "Keep believing in the impossible, Scott. Okay? Just keep believing."

When they got home, Cal helped her father stack wood into a neat cord.

"You're good at that," he said.

"When Mom's better, can we use some of this wood to make a big bonfire in the yard like we used to do?"

"Definitely," Dad said, winking. "We'll make it a party. Invite all the neighbors."

"That would be nice."

Later, they went inside. Dad had already patched the fist-size hole. As he sanded the spackle, Wildcat came to watch. Cal knew he was feeling better when he began making his gurgly-purring sounds.

When you're done with that, he seemed to say, *can you trouble yourself to fix me my dinner? I'm starving.* He began to lick a paw. *And no more sardines. I've had enough of those.*

Cal painted the wall while her father cut up some chicken and put it on a fancy plate for Wildcat.

Now, this is what I'm talking about, Wildcat seemed to say as he gobbled up his supper.

"That cat is an old soul," her father said. "I swear, it's like he's really talking, and I can understand what he's saying."

As if on cue, Wildcat looked up at him and made his gurgly-purring sound as if to say, *Of course, I'm really talking to you! What did you think I was doing? Yodeling?*

Dad burst out laughing.

Right then, watching her dad with Wildcat, Cal felt a smile tug on her lips. A real smile. An outside smile. For the first time in a long time, she didn't fight it. She joined in until they were both laughing so hard Cal had tears in her eyes. The good kind.

"Oh, Wildcat," she finally said. "What would I do without you?"

After dinner and dishes, Dad lit the woodstove for the first time that fall. Then he checked to see if the wall had dried. When it was ready, Cal hung the family photo in its brand-new frame.

Later, when she couldn't keep her eyes open any longer, Cal headed to bed. Wildcat followed, leaping up next to her and making himself comfortable on his new pillow.

Cal got under the covers and closed her eyes. For the first time in a long time, she welcomed sleep, letting her body drift into the darkness of her dreams.

Once again she found herself in the long white corridor.

Cal is immediately inside the current, but this time she doesn't fight it. Instead, she lets it carry her toward the mirror.

She is ready to confront the unearthly white face.

Squinting, she watches as the image sharpens and blurs. Sharpens and blurs.

The face with the hollow eyes is looking straight at her, and for the first time, Cal recognizes it for what it is.

"You?" Cal says. "I'm not afraid of YOU!"

She reaches out and lifts the mirror from the wall, so they're face-to-face. Eyeball to eye socket.

"You are not going to frighten me anymore!" Cal shouts.

The eye sockets grow large.

"You are weak, and I am strong!"

The image sharpens and blurs. Sharpens and blurs.

"I am Calliope Scott, and I'm not going to let you scare me anymore!"

And with that, Cal throws the mirror on the ground, letting it smash into a million shards. Then she turns and begins walking back down the corridor, feeling light as a feather because she has finally destroyed the thing that was destroying her.

She's shattered her own fear.

Chapter 27

Six Weeks Later

"Okay, are we ready to go live?"

Cal stood in front of Demsky's Market, except it wasn't called that anymore. After she'd come up with the perfect name and shared it with Paloma, a new sign hung over the door:

> Welcome to Stardust
> Bleakerville's *other* hidden magic

Paloma stood next to the sign with News-8 reporter Amita Singh and a cameraperson.

Word spread fast in Bleakerville, and it seemed as if

everyone in town had come to be part of the grand opening of the new community swap shop.

Cal scanned the crowd, spotting some of her classmates. Abner Dunlop was there, wearing his apron. Luis Baez was talking with Ms. Adelman. Cal had been spending time with Luis after school, and he'd mentioned that he'd be helping Paloma out at the shop too.

Mr. Lopez caught Cal's eye and gave her a thumbs-up. She waved back.

The Bee Girls hovered at the back of the crowd. When they saw Cal, Lexi smirked before whispering something to Tonia.

That's okay, Cal thought. She'd come prepared. She walked toward them.

They scanned her up and down as she pulled Lexi's pink sweatshirt from her backpack.

"Here, Lexi," she said, handing it to her. "I washed it, so it's nice and clean. I know I shouldn't have taken it, but I want you to know that it kept me warm when I was on the mountain, and I'm grateful for that. Anyway, I'm sorry I took it without asking. It won't happen again."

"Oh, please, Cal," Lexi said, tossing the sweatshirt at Tonia. "You want us to believe you climbed the spire?"

"You can believe or not believe—that's your problem,

not mine." Cal smiled an outside smile. "I know the truth." With that, she made her way back through the crowd to find her parents.

Dad had brought camp chairs. He and Mom were sitting in them at the edge of the crowd. Mom still looked small in her puffy winter coat, but there was color in her cheeks, and she was getting stronger every day. Cal leaned in between them.

"She's late," Cal said. "What if she misses it?"

"Mrs. Demsky left to pick her and Mali up from the bus station an hour ago," Mom said. "They should be here any minute."

The cameraperson called out, "Five, four . . ." before raising his hand to count down with his fingers, three, two, one. He pointed at the news anchor who was standing next to Paloma.

"They're starting, Cal! Go, go, go," Mom said, smiling.

Cal moved near the front.

Amita Singh looked into the camera while speaking into a microphone. "I'm here in Bleakerville with Dr. Paloma Demsky, owner of the new Stardust. Dr. Demsky, can you tell us about your shop?"

"Hi, Amita, thanks for having us! Stardust is a way for our community to come together and help one another." She looked around the crowd. "I grew up in Bleakerville,

282

and I've returned to keep the tradition my father began with his store, Demsky's Market."

"And what tradition is that?"

"We're a small community that's seen a decline in industry, especially during COVID. After so many people lost jobs, my father wanted to make sure everyone had what they needed."

"Can you give us an example?"

"Well, it really was the community who started things. Many people wanted to help their neighbors, but they didn't know how. Then Miss Bamina and Miss McAllister brought in homemade canned goods to share. What they did became contagious. Jorge Lopez brought paper products. My mom made pies and soups. The list goes on and on. Some neighbors even came up with their own disinfectant recipes to share."

The camera panned the crowd as Amita said, "Wow, what a great example of neighbors helping neighbors."

"This shop is my way of expanding Pop's work while continuing my own research."

"Yes, such an unusual combination. Tell us about that."

Paloma stared at the peak of the spire. "Simply put—I am researching the magic of micrometeorites— otherwise known as stardust."

The reporter's eyebrows went up. "Many of us are aware of the legend of Mount Meteorite, but"—she chuckled—"I thought you were a scientist."

"I certainly am, with a PhD in mineralogy. I study micrometeorites—the very real particles that travel through our solar system to earth. Really, Amita, they are everywhere—you might even have some in your hair right now."

The news anchor absently brushed her hair with her hand, then laughed again.

"Bleakerville is actually the perfect place to conduct my research because of the extraterrestrial visitors that landed here more than fifty years ago."

The cameraperson turned to film the spire. Cal looked at it, feeling the same spark she felt whenever she was on the mountain.

"No one's ever proved that the light seen above the mountain was from another world," Amita said.

"But they have! Let me introduce you to my friends." Paloma squinted into the crowd. "There you are! Rosine, come on up here."

Cal's heart practically leapt out of her chest when she saw her friend standing on the edge of the crowd with Mrs. Demsky and Mali.

"Cal, where are you?" Paloma called.

Cal and Rosine exchanged grins before making their way toward Paloma.

"Not only did these two ladies summit the spire," Paloma continued, "they also gathered a rich sample of stardust—cosmic particles that traveled for more than four billion years before arriving here in Bleakerville."

Amita scanned the girls skeptically before her gaze shifted back to the spire.

"You ladies climbed that?"

Rosine and Cal nodded.

Amita shook her head. "Why?"

"It's hard to explain." Cal looked at Rosine, then into the crowd. How could she say all that their journey had meant? And then it hit her—why Mr. Demsky and Mr. Lopez had kept their secret.

"I guess you could say we were each looking for something different, but something similar as well," Cal said.

"Okay," Amita said. "What was the thing in common?"

Rosine grinned. "The magic, of course."

"And did you find it? Is the legend true?"

"Definitely," Cal said.

Rosine nodded. "One hundred percent."

"Can you share with the audience how you can prove that?"

The girls looked at each other. "Nope, we can't."

The reporter looked disappointed.

"But we can share this advice—go climb a mountain. And that mountain, it could be Mount Meteorite, or another one," Rosine said.

"Or maybe not a mountain at all," Cal said. "Maybe just face a problem straight on."

"Each of us has our own mountains to climb," Rosine said.

"Oh, yeah, one more piece of advice," Cal added. "When you set off, make sure you do it with a friend. A true friend. Because if you do, that's when the impossible becomes possible."

"Do you really believe that?" the news anchor asked.

Rosine grinned and Cal couldn't help smiling too. She looked into the audience and caught her mother's eye.

"Totally," she said.

Chapter 28

After the crowd dispersed, Paloma thanked Rosine and Cal again. "I have a feeling that my father was waiting for the two of you to bring the magic to me, and by magic, I mean this place."

Cal grinned as her parents walked over with Mali.

"I'm so glad you were able to come today, Mali," Paloma said. "I know it's far for you, and you're busy with work and school."

"It was important to Rosine, so I made the time." Mali nodded. "We are sisters first. We will always be there for each other."

"Mali," Rosine said, "Cal and I want to go to the mountain for a quick visit. Is that okay?"

"The bus to Hartford leaves at six. You won't stay long?"

"No, we'll come back soon. I promise."

"Yes, but what will I do, eh?" Mali asked, wrapping her scarf tight around her neck. "It's freezing out here, and it looks like it will snow."

Cal's mom linked arms with her. "You'll join us for hot cider and a warm fire. Mrs. Demsky and Paloma are coming over too."

Mali smiled. "Thank you. I will enjoy that very much."

Cal's mom winked at the girls as she tugged Mali toward home.

"I'm going to help Paloma lock up and then I'll be right over," Mrs. Demsky called, waving.

On the way up Mountain Road, Cal watched the ribbon of smoke curl from their own chimney. The black shutters she'd helped her father paint glistened, smart and neat. She couldn't help but admire the cord of wood she'd helped stack.

Her father had used some of the wood to make a bonfire on their front lawn. He'd set camp chairs in a circle around it. Mom and Mali took a seat as Dad lit the fire.

"Not too long, okay, girls?" Mom called.

Before they could answer, there was a squeal from Mali.

Cal turned to see that Wildcat had leapt onto Mali's shoulder. He brushed his cheek against hers as if to say, *Here you are! I've been looking for you. I never did have a chance to thank you properly!*

Mali laughed. "You are one tough cat, my friend," she said.

Dad grinned. "We weren't sure if he would stay with us or try to go back to the mountain."

"It is the only home he's ever known," Mom added.

Wildcat crawled down Mali's arm and sat on her lap. He purred deeply, clearly enjoying the fire and the back scratch.

Mali laughed again. "He looks very happy here," she said. "I'm sure everything must have seemed new and strange to him at first, but I think this place is starting to feel like home to him now." She turned toward Rosine. "What do you think, sister?" she asked.

"One hundred percent," Rosine said, smiling.

As Dad brought steaming hot cider out to Mom and Mali, Cal and Rosine made their way up Mountain Road. Soon the pavement steepened, then narrowed, then turned to dirt. When they came to the yellow sign, Cal high-fived it, leaving its gong-like vibration behind as they ducked beneath the forest canopy.

"I think this is the first time I've ever *walked* up the mountain," Cal said.

"Well, I like this speed," Rosine said. "It's the only way to see everything. The forest looks so different than it did a month and a half ago."

"Yeah. The mountain is always changing," Cal said.

"Mali and I were so happy to hear your mother's surgery went well," Rosine said.

Cal leapt over a small root. "Yes, she's still healing . . . but getting stronger every day."

"What will the doctors do next?"

"Scans and then radiation. Also, there's a new treatment they want to try." Cal looked up. "The most important thing is that Mom promised me that she'll tell me what's next—as much as she knows it." She took a deep breath. "And I promised Mom that when I'm worried about something or I have questions, I'm going to come to her instead of running away. And not just to my mom, but Dad too. I know it's not going to be easy, but we decided that whatever comes next, we'll face it together."

"I'll be with you too," Rosine said. "Even if I'm not actually here."

Cal put a hand to her waist as if touching the invisible rope and grinned. "I'm counting on it."

When the well-worn path veered left, Cal and Rosine turned right.

"How about you and Mali?" Cal asked. "How's it going in the city?"

"I like my new school and my teachers." She sighed. "Still, sometimes it gets lonely, you know?"

Cal nodded. She knew. "Next time you feel lonely, don't forget I'm on the other end of that rope too."

"Always." Rosine grinned. "The good news for me is that I joined a soccer club. I'll be playing every day after school."

"That's great!" Cal said. "Hey, did you ask Mali about coming for Thanksgiving next week?"

"She already told Mrs. Demsky yes, we will come."

"Yay! You guys will make it extra special."

"Oh, and Mali has the best news."

"What?"

"She started volunteering at an animal shelter after work. Wildcat reminded her how much she loved helping animals. She's even taking veterinarian classes at the community college."

"That's awesome!" Cal said.

"How's school for you?" Rosine asked.

"Good. Of course, it would be better if you were

there," Cal said, nudging Rosine with her shoulder. "When I returned the harnesses and shoes I took, Ms. Adelman said my punishment was to help her start an after-school climbing program."

Rosine laughed. "That's not a punishment."

"Nope." Cal laughed. "And remember that kid, Luis? We're working together." She shrugged. "He's really nice. It's actually a lot of fun."

The girls continued through the woods until they came to the pencil-thin ridge. One after the other, they shimmied across, climbing over Wildcat's boulder, then jumping down so they stood in front of the cave.

The world was silent and still. Snowflakes began to drift.

"Ahh," Rosine said. "It's so pretty. Like sugar being sifted from the sky."

"Yeah," Cal agreed. "So that was kind of weird, before. Talking about the mountain with all those strangers. I don't know . . . it felt like they wanted the magic to be something it wasn't," Cal said.

"Do you think that's why Mr. Demsky and Mr. Lopez never told anyone what they saw on the spire?" Rosine asked.

"Definitely. I think they knew it wouldn't matter

what they said. Same as it didn't matter what we told the TV people."

Cal gazed up at the spire. Inside the snowy day, it appeared gray and somber.

"Remember how Mr. Demsky told us that if we *believed*, that's when we'd find the magic?" Cal said. "I didn't understand what we were supposed to believe *in* until we scaled the spire."

"And what was that?" Rosine asked.

"We needed to believe in ourselves."

"This is true. As my mother always told us, *Maisha ni mapambano, ili upate amani utapitia mengi.*"

"Hey! Amani! You just said that word—*amani*." Cal raised an eyebrow. "The word your mother sewed into the handkerchief."

"Yes," Rosine said.

"You know, you never told me what *amani* means."

"I didn't?"

Cal shook her head. "No, but I think I figured it out anyway."

As snowflakes continued to fall, Cal gazed at the town below. Layered in a fresh coat of winter white, it looked as if it had dressed for the occasion.

She let her gaze follow Mountain Road, until she

found her own home. She could see Dad, Mom, Mali, Mrs. Demsky, and Paloma sitting around the giant bonfire. Its flames had grown so tall, they seemed to touch the sky.

Like fire on ice.

Even from halfway up Mount Meteorite, Cal could feel its warmth.

Staring into its light, Cal knew she was strong enough to get through whatever came next. She had learned that the magic was never something she needed to find. Just like stardust, she was made of it.

Cal leaned into her friend. For the first time in a long time, she didn't want to run away. She wanted to stand still and be.

"Everything is as it should be," she said.

Rosine leaned back. "Amani," she whispered.

"Peace."

Author's Note

On a school visit, I talked to a teacher who expressed the need for more middle grade books about kids dealing with a parent's cancer diagnosis. Since both of my parents had cancer, and my own kids had to cope with my own cancer battles, I thought I might bring a unique perspective to this difficult subject.

Having been on both sides of the cancer coin, I believe the more difficult role belongs to the person helplessly watching a loved one face this disease. Kids of cancer patients are forced to deal with so many unknowns. Without notice, parents can be whisked out of the house, sometimes in the middle of the night, due to a spiked fever or other medical emergency. Some kids are unable to see their parent for weeks or even months at a time. Often, kids have no idea what's coming next because even the doctors aren't sure. Maybe the hardest part is watching Mom or Dad morph into an unrecognizable stranger.

Cal's story doesn't answer all the questions a parent's

cancer diagnosis can ignite, but I hope it does this: I hope it lets children know they are not alone. I hope it reminds readers to find a friend to share their worries with. I hope it encourages kids to reach out to an adult when they are scared or confused or sad. Most of all, I hope it reminds each of us that we are so much stronger than we know.

Just as Rosine's mom wished peace for her daughters, my wish is that within Cal and Rosine's story, anyone facing their own impossible will find peace too.

A Note from
Ndengo Gladys Mwilelo

My name is Ndengo Gladys Mwilelo. I was born in the Democratic Republic of the Congo (DRC), which is the second largest country in Africa.

For many years, DRC has experienced war and conflict. This caused my family to flee our home when I was two years old, leaving behind family, friends, and everything we owned. In search of safety, we crossed Lake Tanganyika by boat into Burundi, where we lived as refugees for thirteen years before coming to the United States.

Working on this book was important to me because I feel like the experiences Rosine faced are usually only shared with adults. I want kids to learn about refugees in the language that they understand the most—from another child's words.

I want readers to know that although DRC has undergone much hardship for many years, the Congolese people are resilient. They are kind and loving. We show our pride by displaying our country flag everywhere and playing our famous music, rumba, which Congo-Kinshasa is known for.

Although I was a refugee in Burundi, it was my second home. Often, I was treated as an outsider there, even though it's the only place I can remember in Africa. Then we came to the United States, and it was like starting all over again. I had to learn a new language and adapt to a new culture.

It would have been easy for me to feel sorry for myself each time I had to deal with a new situation. Instead, I chose to find something valuable inside each challenge and move forward. With each success, I learned more about myself and the world around me.

I love that although Rosine and Cal are from different continents, with completely different backgrounds and upbringings, they find connection and friendship. I believe Rosine learns from Cal that people everywhere have problems and that even kids from America are not immune from trouble. Rosine sees past Cal's anger and sadness because she understands these emotions come from fear. She teaches Cal to face that fear, and through their journey, they both find peace. I think this is the most important lesson of all—as humans, we must love one another.

By sharing my own experiences and background, I

want readers to know that no matter what challenges they face, there is always hope. In my life, I have faced many obstacles. In conquering them, I have found strength. Like most people, I still face difficulties, but it is different now because I've learned how powerful I am. I hope that when kids read this book, they will recognize their own power too.

Meet a Real Stardust Hunter

As Dr. Paloma Demsky says, "Stardust is real, Cal. And that's a fact. Whether it's magical or not? Well, that's up to you."

Stardust—or micrometeorites—are micrometeoroids that have survived entry through our atmosphere to land on the earth. Approximately one thousand six hundred tons of this cosmic dust land on the earth each year. This equates to approximately one micrometeorite per square meter per year. Some micrometeorites are older than the earth itself and can include actual remnants of our solar system's birth.

Although stardust is literally all around us, until recently, most scientists believed it was impossible to find it in urban areas. That is, until a Norwegian jazz musician and amateur scientist proved them wrong.

When Jon Larsen noticed a speck of dust on his patio table that hadn't been there only a moment ago, he became intrigued. Studying this tiny granule, which was about the size of the period at the end of this sentence, he discovered it was a micrometeorite that had traveled across the universe to land in his backyard.

Through his work and his books *On the Trail of Stardust* and *In Search of Stardust,* Jon has inspired even more scientists—and ordinary citizens—to search for these extraterrestrial particles.

One such scientist is Mr. Scott Peterson, a stardust hunter in Minnesota, who continues to discover micrometeorites on roofs in urban areas. He shares his findings on his website, micro-meteorites.com.

Like Larsen, Scott Peterson has worked tirelessly to spread the word of the magic of micrometeorites. He was instrumental to my understanding of the subject matter, generously and patiently sharing his knowledge and enthusiasm, while answering my endless questions.

Here is what he says about how you (*under the supervision of an adult*) can find stardust too . . . and that is magical in and of itself!

Hi, Mr. Peterson, thank you for talking with us! What equipment do you need to collect micrometeorites?
You'll need a powerful magnet (like a fishing magnet), two Ziploc bags, a dustpan and brush, a 20X–2000X

microscope, sieves (I use sizes no. 40, 60, and 80), and tweezers.

Where do you go to find micrometeorites?

I start by finding large, flat vinyl roofs. (Schools are often an excellent option!) Once I get permission to access the roof, I look for areas where dirt and debris have accumulated. Generally, water from rainfall or melting snow will carry micrometeorites to drainage and lower areas of the roof.

How do you collect a sample?

I use a powerful magnet wrapped tight in a Ziploc bag and a dustpan brush to sweep up the loose dirt. I hover the magnet over the material so that it picks up anything magnetic. Most of this will be terrestrial material such as rust or iron filings, but chances are you'll have gathered micrometeorites too! I then transfer the material I've collected into a "mother bag" to bring home for cleaning.

Once you've collected a sample, what happens next?

At home I wash the material to get rid of the small particulates and any organic material. Once the material is dry, I sift the granules with a series of sieves, starting with the one with the largest holes and ending with the one with the smallest holes, until I'm left with the tiniest granules—specifically, those between 0.180 mm and 0.425 mm because most micrometeorites fall in the range of 0.2 to 0.4 mm. Once the sample is clean, I take another magnet and hover it over the material to collect all magnetic material, including the possible micrometeorites. I transfer this material to a microscope slide, and I look at it under my microscope using sweeping motions, combing every inch of material and studying each grain of dirt. I'm looking for roundish and blackish spheres. They don't have to be perfectly round—most aren't—and they don't have to be black, but this is a good technique to start until you can pick them out right away.

What do you do after you've determined which grains are potentially micrometeorites?
Once I have identified the possible micrometeorites, I will either place them on a micro-fossil slide with a white Post-it note upside down to store them, or I will transfer them to a Scanning Electron Microscope (SEM) sample holder with black carbon tape. I usually try and take some images, and then I bring the micrometeorites to the University of Minnesota for analysis and imaging.

The last and current step is to gather as much data

as possible, and try and contribute to science with any interesting findings.

What do you love most about micrometeorite hunting?

Everything about micrometeorite hunting is lovely from climbing onto roofs and getting dirty to spending time discovering them under the microscope. I've been fortunate enough to meet many people, from all over the world, who share my interest in micrometeorites, and I am excited to continue spreading the word about their existence. I guess what I love most is the thrill of spotting them hidden inside a pile of dirt. It's exciting every time. Even after almost two thousand micrometeorites, I still love finding each and every one.

Is there anything else you'd like to share with kids who want to try finding stardust?

I think there are two things I'd like to share. First, that this can be done by anyone! There are micrometeorites all around us just waiting to be found. Second, and most importantly, be patient and persistent. It might be difficult to find them at first, but as with anything, if you don't give up, you will succeed. Your reward will be a tiny piece of the cosmos all for you.

Acknowledgments

Cal and Rosine's story is about facing adversity and fear, and finding peace and strength in the struggle. For Rosine, it was the everyday challenge of being a refugee in America and recovering from devastating loss. For Cal, it was dealing with a parent's cancer diagnosis.

I begin each book as a student of the story I'm trying to write. Fortunately, I have had many teachers along the way.

Over the course of two years, I consulted with Ndengo Gladys Mwilelo for this book. As always, Gladys spoke bravely and honestly about her experiences coming to both Burundi and the United States as a refugee. She read multiple versions of the manuscript, offering her advice and exquisite wisdom, and infusing her strength and beauty into the story. I am so grateful Gladys continues her important work with Integrated Refugee and Immigrant Services (irisct.org), where she passionately and tirelessly offers her powerful voice in service to our world and its citizens.

Consolata Ndayishimiye also read an early draft of this book and provided valuable advice about her experiences in Burundi and coming to the United States.

Serendipity brought me to several experts who, because of their passion for a subject, were incredibly generous with their time and talent. *Please know that any errors I made translating their knowledge into story falls squarely on me.*

Dr. Ralph Yulo planted the seed for this book with three magical words: "You are stardust." Whether reciting facts, or one of the hundreds of poems he knows by heart, Dr. Yulo brings us mere mortals to the intersection of science and faith—a magical place indeed.

Scott Peterson maintains the website micro-meteorites .com. He patiently taught me about space, meteors, and stardust, and even sent me a micrometeorite that I can't wait to show kids on school visits! Scott vetted scenes about micrometeorites, catching my mistakes and helping this story ring true.

Kim V. Fendrich, Department of Earth and Planetary Sciences, American Museum of Natural History, taught me about stellar nucleosynthesis and supernovae, and vetted all things extraterrestrial.

Although hiking through mountains has been a longtime passion for me, I never rock climbed until I began this book. A note to readers: *Rock climbing is an inherently dangerous activity.* I would have never attempted this without help from experts. Fortunately, climbing continues to grow as a sport, and there are many gyms and guides to help "newbs" like me get started. Two such organizations are Stone Age Rock Gym in Manchester, Connecticut, and Sunrise Mountain Guides in Stowe, Vermont. Through their many kindnesses, these professionals have demonstrated firsthand how welcoming the climbing community truly is.

Alex Sargent and Walt Ward of Sunrise Mountain Guides taught my family and me to rock climb at Smugglers' Notch, Stowe, Vermont. Months later, Alex, an expert climber, backcountry skier, and former instructor at the US Army Mountain Warfare School, read climbing scenes and generously shared his knowledge. I am incredibly grateful for his help and advice.

Kevin West, owner, and Bill Fleming, manager, at Stone Age Rock Gym taught me about climbing (patiently!) and explained (more than once!) about knots, climbing technique, gear, and most of all, how to be safe and have fun. Kevin also read numerous scenes, helping to ensure accuracy.

John Zulick of Boy Scout Troop 92 in Ashford, Connecticut, taught me about campfire safety and showed me how to turn a flint's spark into a roaring fire. (The hollowed-out oranges filled with brownie dough that we cooked in the hot coals weren't too shabby either, Deb Zulick!)

A book is never written in isolation, and I am beholden to the many talented readers and writers who provided advice on early drafts. Thank you to:

My writing partner in crime, Bette Anne Rieth. No matter how many words I have at my disposal, they aren't enough to express my gratitude to you, my talented friend.

The fabulous Nancy Tandon, Holly Howley, and Eileen Washburn. You guys made the journey up the mountain way less rocky and way more fun. Your dedication to creating beautiful stories, and the hard work you put in to make that happen, inspires me more than you'll ever know.

Kathryn Fitzgerald, sixth-grade teacher at Crystal Lake School in Ellington, Connecticut. Mrs. Fitzgerald generously read this story to her students and provided me with valuable advice on rocks and mountain formations.

Andrea Adelman, Paloma Morrison, and Cassie Morrison were kind enough to read an early manuscript and provide important feedback.

Like Cal's mom, I had cancer twice. I want to give a

special thank-you to the doctors and nurses at Memorial Sloan Kettering Cancer Center and the Smilow Cancer Hospital at Yale New Haven Care Center who brought me through my cancer journeys. Each day health care professionals wake up, look cancer in the eye, and take on the impossible. I have full confidence they will ultimately prevail, and cancer will be a disease of the past.

An extra loud shout-out goes to my oncologist, Dr. Mary Louise Keohan at the MSKCC Sarcoma Center. Like Rosine, you are the superhero of never giving up.

Jesse Flaherty runs the Livestrong program for cancer thrivers and survivors at the YMCA in Ellington, Connecticut. Since my first diagnosis, Jesse has been a friend, adviser, and trainer. Thank you, Jesse, for making me, and so many others, physically and mentally strong.

Viola Wiggins took a heavy weight from my shoulders with her dedication to health care and her kindness.

Great books wouldn't exist without the professionals who believe in them. Thank you to:

The entire team at Farrar, Straus and Giroux, whose passion for beautiful literature enriches our lives, especially Janine O'Malley and Melissa Warten, who always see and bring out the best in stories. Wildcat wants to add a *gurgly-purr thank-you* for rescuing him from a winter spent inside a frozen cave!

Rich Deas captures beauty and emotion in one glorious cover after another with his illustration, and Veronica Mang with her jacket design. Lindsay Wagner and Lelia Mander for your precise and thoughtful editing.

Stacey Glick at Dystel, Goderich & Bourret, who keeps this train on the tracks.

Last but not least, thank you to my family, Paul, Andrew, and Sophia Ferruolo, and my mother, Barbara Zulick. Each and every day you make the impossible possible.